I0671767

Symmetry

by

Joyce Scarbrough

This is a work of fiction. Names, characters, places, and incidents are either the product of the author's imagination or are used fictitiously, and any resemblance to actual persons living or dead, business establishments, events, or locales, is entirely coincidental.

Symmetry

COPYRIGHT © 2014 by Joyce Scarbrough

All rights reserved. No part of this book may be used or reproduced in any manner whatsoever without written permission of the author or The Wild Rose Press, Inc. except in the case of brief quotations embodied in critical articles or reviews.
Contact Information: info@thewildrosepress.com

Cover Art by *Debbie Taylor*

The Wild Rose Press, Inc.
PO Box 708
Adams Basin, NY 14410-0708
Visit us at www.thewildrosepress.com

Publishing History
First Champagne Rose Edition, 2014
Print ISBN 978-1-62830-221-9
Digital ISBN 978-1-62830-222-6

Published in the United States of America

Jess always woke a second before she could complete the castration. Curses, foiled again.

She blinked at the red numbers projected onto her ceiling by the clock on her nightstand—4:23 a.m. Plenty of time to go back to sleep and finish the job, but she knew it was useless. She'd only end up dreaming about giving birth to a canned ham or grocery shopping in her pajamas, and Lee's manhood would escape the knife again.

She snuggled against the body pillow occupying his place beside her in bed and got an indignant *rowl* from the Siamese cat curled up there. Jess smiled at the thought of what Lee would say about letting Ming sleep with her and decided maybe she'd tell him he'd been replaced by his feline nemesis when she saw him at the meeting later that morning.

She fell asleep reminding herself of how much better off she was without her two-timing, cat-hating, conceited jerk of a husband, and she dreamed he made love to her on the conference table at work, castration the furthest thing from her mind.

God, she hated him.

Praise for *SYMMETRY*

2011 EPIC Award Finalist in General Fiction

"*SYMMETRY* is a wonderful book! Both evocative and touching in its depiction of a difficult period in a marriage, it also conveys a sense of transformation and discovery as the main character, Jess, discovers there is real help for a hair-pulling disorder she has. The story is one of healing, in both an interpersonal relationship and in living with trichotillomania, an often chronic and potentially debilitating compulsive behavior. Jess is a hero of mine!"

~Christina Pearson, founding director of the Trichotillomania Learning Center

"Joyce Scarbrough has written this story of a troubled woman and a crumbling marriage with sensitivity and grace. It's a helpful, hopeful, and ultimately uplifting novel. Highly recommended for mature adolescents and adult readers."

~Laurel Johnson, Midwest Book Reviews

"I enjoyed *SYMMETRY* for the writing. The characters pulled me right in and kept me engaged. I felt for Jessica and her turmoil. Learning about TTM, which I had no knowledge of before opening the book, was a bonus. It's a recommended read for those interested in romance, those who are somehow touched by trichotillomania, and those who simply enjoy a well-told story."

~Lisa Haselton's Book Reviews

Dedication

Dedicated to all the people suffering alone
who don't even know that
what they do has a name.
You are not defective, damaged, or mentally ill,
and you are worthy of
love and understanding.

AUTHOR'S NOTE

I gave Jess trichotillomania because I have it myself and wanted to raise awareness of it in the general population. However, I want to make it clear that this book isn't intended to educate anyone who needs treatment. There are many fine reference books available to do that, and they can all be found on the Trichotillomania Learning Center's Web site at http://www.trich.org.

I've been asked why I decided to include a topic like hair-pulling in a novel instead of telling my own story about dealing with it in a book of non-fiction. The answer to that is twofold. First, I have TTM only to the degree that Jess has it, so it's not a major problem for me and certainly not interesting enough for an entire book about it. Second, I figured that the only people who read non-fiction books about TTM are people who already know what it is, and my goal is to raise awareness about it in the rest of the population.

I hope you enjoy this book for the story, but I also hope you gain some empathy for the millions of people like Jess and Cara. Teach your children not to make fun of their peers who may have missing hair, eyebrows or eyelashes. You wouldn't let them laugh at a cancer patient or a diabetic, would you? TTM is no less of a physical ailment.

~Joyce Scarbrough

Chapter One

Jess always woke a second before she could complete the castration. Curses, foiled again.

She blinked at the red numbers projected onto her ceiling by the clock on her nightstand—4:23 a.m. Plenty of time to go back to sleep and finish the job, but she knew it was useless. She'd only end up dreaming about giving birth to a canned ham or grocery shopping in her pajamas, and Lee's manhood would escape the knife again.

She snuggled against the body pillow occupying his place beside her in bed and got an indignant *rowl* from the Siamese cat curled up there. Jess smiled at the thought of what Lee would say about letting Ming sleep with her and decided maybe she'd tell him he'd been replaced by his feline nemesis when she saw him at the meeting later that morning.

She fell asleep reminding herself of how much better off she was without her two-timing, cat-hating, conceited jerk of a husband, and she dreamed he made love to her on the conference table at work, castration the furthest thing from her mind.

God, she hated him.

****

Five hours later, Jess sat across from Lee in the conference room at the *Espanola Times* and tried to focus on Thad Crandall's weekly lecture about

1

deadlines. If she hadn't known better, she would have thought Lee knew what she'd dreamed about him from the way he kept nudging her with his foot under the table and flashing that damn blond-Adonis smile at her.

She tried to suppress the dream images of his face over hers, but every time she looked at him, her mind became a private movie screen featuring the world premiere of *Position: Impossible*. Shackled as she was with a redhead's proclivity for blushing, she knew he noticed her agitation and probably thought it was from simply being near him.

As soon as the meeting adjourned, she tried to avoid him by fleeing down the hall toward the copyediting room, but he waylaid her just before she reached her desk.

"Wait, Jess. Did you get my message about coming over Friday? We need to talk."

"Talk to my lawyer. I don't have anything to say to you." She took a step back and tried to walk around him, but he held on to her arm.

"We both know you don't hate me, so you might as well quit trying to act like you do."

She smiled, but her eyes were an angry green. "As I've pointed out to you countless times in your copy, the proper expression is act *as if* you do. And you lost all claim to giving me orders when you decided to trade your marriage for a night in Silicone Heaven. Remember?" She freed her arm and pushed past him to sit at her desk.

He leaned over and lowered his voice. "You can't divorce me over one night of drunken stupidity."

"Just watch me. And the stupidity is chronic."

"Damn it, Jess. How many times do I have to say

I'm sorry?"

"Nine trillion, seven hundred fifty-three billion—"

"Stop it. I'm trying to fix things and you're making jokes."

She smiled again. "No, I'm completely serious. Your inability to distinguish between humor and sincerity is another reason I'm divorcing you. Now go away. I have work to do."

"Okay, fine." He moved her stapler to the middle of her desk, turned her calendar to the wrong day and shook several paper clips onto her blotter from the magnetic holder. "Here's a few things to keep you busy in case you run out of stuff to nitpick in my articles." He tweaked her chin and winked before walking away.

She glared at his infuriatingly broad shoulders and struggled to leave the items askew until he was gone. He paused in the doorway and turned to smile at her.

"Go ahead and put 'em back. I know it's killing you."

She held up four fingers. "Can you read through camouflage, Lee?"

He laughed and winked again. "See you Friday at seven."

Jess looked around the room to see how much attention they'd attracted. Most of her coworkers were doing their best to look as if they hadn't seen or heard anything, but her best friend Deb Landry was practically hurdling the desks between them, her long blonde curls bouncing in testimony to her agitation.

"What happens Friday at seven?" Deb demanded. "Don't you *dare* let that lying dog charm you into taking him back!"

Jess sighed as she restored order to her desk. "I

3

have no intention of taking him back, but he's right. We have things to discuss."

"Like what?" Deb swiped a chair from a neighboring desk and pulled it beside Jess. "You mean alimony?"

"No, I don't want any money from him, but we do have some joint property."

Deb looked skeptical. "He didn't act like he had property division in mind. I wouldn't trust him, Jess."

"Don't worry, his lame attempts at flirting only remind me of how many women he's probably been practicing on behind my back. I'm immune to him." Maybe if she kept saying it, it would eventually be true.

"Good, because you deserve much better than Lee Cassady, even if he is drop-dead gorgeous."

Jess rolled her eyes. "Thanks, Deb. You're a big help."

Just before lunchtime, a bouquet of carnations arrived for Jess with a note from Lee that read: *I'm sorry, I'm sorry, I'm sorry. How many does that leave?* Jess gave the flowers to their septuagenarian food page editor and told her she must have a secret admirer in the sports department. When Clara said she hoped it was the hunky blond with the cute butt, Jess told her not to get her hopes up because she'd heard that guy was gay.

"He couldn't even spring for roses?" Deb said while they ate calzones for lunch at Guido's. "Lousy cheapskate."

Jess stirred her iced tea with the straw. "Carnations are my favorite. I'm surprised he remembered."

Deb's eyes narrowed as she wiped marinara sauce from her mouth with her napkin. "You're really starting to worry me with all these wistful looks and lack of malice when you talk about him. Must I remind you what a scumbag he is?"

"Of course not. He's maggot phlegm as far as I'm concerned. You know that."

"I thought I did, but now I'm not so sure." Deb pushed a recalcitrant curl behind her ear. "And it's not as if you don't have a history of forgiving him for his many faults."

Jess gave up trying to eat and pushed away her plate. "Yeah, well, sleeping with a bimbo at a sportswriters' convention is a bit more serious than putting the empty milk carton back in the refrigerator or leaving the toilet seat up. I won't be forgiving him this time."

"Great," Deb said. "Because I can't wait for Thad to find out his precious Hearst Journalism Award winner couldn't write his way out of an essay contest without your help."

Jess's hand toyed with the hair at her temple. "That's not true, Deb. Lee's good at the kind of writing he does. I just make it printable."

"See what I mean?" Deb threw down her napkin. "After everything the scuzzball has done, you still take up for him. And leave your hair alone."

Jess stuck her hand under her thigh. "Don't nag, Deb. About Lee or anything else. I have everything under control."

Deb sighed heavily enough for it to be a statement. "I'll believe that when you don't come to work next Monday wearing your wedding ring again and missing half your hair." When Jess turned away, Deb sighed again. "The prescription you got for stress isn't working?"

Jess kept her gaze on the sidewalk outside the window. "I hate the way it made me feel—or not feel, to be more accurate. Like being injected with emotional Novocain."

"A lower dose maybe?"

Jess shook her head. "It didn't help anyway, and I decided I don't need drugs to help me deal with stress. I'm an intelligent woman with enough self-control to handle it on my own."

Deb took Jess's hand down from her hair and squeezed it. "Some things you can't control by yourself, sweetie. Don't be ashamed to ask for help from wherever you need it."

When they returned to the office, Jess found a new e-mail message from Lee in her Inbox. She deleted it unread but broke down a few minutes later and read it in the trash folder: *I'm sorry* written continuously for an entire page. She sent him a copy of an employee memo about company e-mail being for business correspondence only, and he replied immediately with a blank message embedded with a .WAV file of Stevie Wonder singing "I Just Called to Say I Love You."

****

When Jess got home at six, Ming met her at the door as usual.

"How's my pretty girl?" Jess picked her up for an affectionate scratch under the chin. "Hey, I brought you a surprise."

Ming purred in response while Jess carried her to the kitchen and opened a can of shrimp for her. While watching her appreciative cat devour her favorite treat, Jess decided this was something else she'd have to make sure Lee heard about. Maybe she'd even let Ming

6

eat shrimp in her lap when Lee came over Friday to discuss the divorce.

Her stomach did its usual acrobatics at the thought of being alone with him for the first time since she'd thrown him out after her call to his hotel room was answered in the middle of the night by a woman's sleepy voice. Grateful for the fury that resurfaced at the memory, Jess assured herself that she hated him enough to continue ignoring his pathetic attempts at reconciliation.

Unless he showed up Friday wearing that damn blue shirt he knew she loved.

With a disgusted sigh over her weakness for the jerk, she put a French bread pizza in the microwave before going into the bedroom to change into her favorite slouch attire: an old T-shirt and flannel lounge pants decorated with frolicking cats. She paused to look in the mirror and pulled out a couple of errant hairs curling in different directions from their auburn buddies nearby, examining them to confirm that they were coarser than they should be before she dropped them into the wastebasket.

See, she had a handle on this hair-pulling thing. She only pulled odd strands that interfered with the symmetry of her hairstyle, and she only pulled one or two at the most. Considering she had enough hair for three people, there was nothing wrong with that.

Halfway through watching the movie she'd rented, she realized her hand had been in her hair for so long that her arm was aching. And when she looked with horror at the thirty or so strands she dropped on the carpet beside her, it became painfully obvious that she wasn't controlling anything.

Chapter Two

"You look tired," Deb said the next morning at the coffee pot in the employee break room.

"Gee, thanks, Deb." Jess added French vanilla creamer to her coffee. "That's always nice to hear."

Deb followed her to their usual table. "Sorry, but it's the truth. And I sure hope you're not losing sleep over that rodent you married."

"No, it had nothing to do with Lee." Jess sat down and pointedly ignored the box of doughnuts calling her name from the next table. "I was online doing research and lost track of time."

"Research on what?"

"Trichotillomania."

"Trick-o-what?" Deb's blue eyes widened. "Sounds like some kind of kinky Wiccan gardening fetish. Wait—are we finally looking to meet some new men?"

Jess laughed. "No, it's compulsive hair pulling, derived from the Greek words for *hair, pull* and...well, the last part is debatable, but I prefer *craving* over the alternatives. I Googled it last night and found lots of info on the Trichotillomania Learning Center Web site."

Deb looked dubious. "Don't you think yours is just a nervous habit from all the stress you've been under lately?"

"I did until I read about it online and recognized myself in the description. And stress can definitely make it harder to control."

Deb reached for the box of doughnuts and bit into a cruller. "How's it treated?"

"It depends on the individual. I'll know more about it after I get the book I ordered by the doctor who's had the most success at treating it." Jess stared into her coffee cup a moment. "Thanks for not being weirded-out by all this, Deb. I know from what I've read that it doesn't mean I'm crazy, but I still don't think I could bring myself to tell anyone about it except you."

Deb squeezed her hand. "What are friends for, sweetie? Besides, the only thing that would make me question your sanity is letting Captain Infidelity back into your life."

Jess shook her head with a laugh. "Exactly how many names do you have for him now?"

Deb shrugged. "Everybody needs a hobby."

When they entered the copyediting room a few minutes later, they saw a balloon bouquet anchored to Jess's desk by a teddy bear holding a heart emblazoned with I'M SORRY.

Deb folded her arms and sighed. "Hey, Jess, do me a favor and Google *punchajerkamania* the next time you're online. I keep getting an uncontrollable urge to hit a certain blond reporter."

****

By the time Friday arrived, Lee had made five more attempts at gaining Jess's forgiveness. They'd all failed, but she had to admire his persistence. For tranquility's sake, she didn't share her appreciative sentiments with Deb when they clocked out together at the end of the day.

"I still think I should come over and chaperone while he's there," Deb said.

"Oh, sure. That would make it go ever so much smoother, considering how well the two of you get along."

"Well, that should tell you something about him right there. He only gets along with women he can flirt with, and his fake charm doesn't work on me. I can see right through his pretty-boy exterior to the slimy worm he is inside."

Jess sighed as they stopped to wait for the elevator. "Well, so can I, so you can stop worrying. I just want to get this over with."

"Did your book arrive yet?" Deb asked. "The one about the hair pulling?"

"Not unless it came today."

"How many pages is it?"

"I'm not sure. Why?"

"I hope it's really thick," Deb said. "Then you can hit Lee over the head with it and write the doctor to tell him how much his book helped you get rid of your stress."

After Jess promised she would call first thing in the morning with a full report, they said goodbye in the parking lot. Jess stopped at Publix on the way home for Ming's shrimp and decided to get herself a quart of cherry vanilla ice cream for after Lee was gone. While she stood in line to check out, she remembered the way he'd looked at her that afternoon when he'd reminded her of their "date" and went back to swap the quart for a half gallon.

Ming made herself scarce after greeting Jess at the

door, as though the cat sensed her enemy's impending arrival. The closer it got to seven o'clock, the more Jess considered joining Ming in her hiding place. If Lee started saying the things he'd been writing to her in notes and e-mail messages all week, she wasn't sure she could maintain the proper level of hatred for him.

She changed into jeans and a caramel-colored sweater that accentuated her modest curves, telling herself it was only to let him see what he was losing. She almost convinced herself it was true while she touched up her makeup and fussed with her hair. Feeling guilty for the five strands she pulled before she was done, she went back to the kitchen and decided to put on a pot of coffee. Lee hated coffee.

As she stirred cream into her first cup, she heard a noise behind her and turned around.

"You shouldn't be drinking that nasty stuff," Lee said. "You'll be up all night."

"Give me your key." She walked toward him with her hand outstretched. "I should've known you wouldn't have the decency not to use it."

Instead of his key, he placed a box from Rommel's Bakery in her hand. "Look, baby. I brought your favorite treat to go with your caffeine addiction. The finest éclairs in the state of Georgia."

He favored her with one of his best smiles—the blue of his eyes a perfect match for the shirt she'd been afraid he would wear—and she knew Deb had been right. She should never have agreed to meet with him alone.

She put the éclairs on the counter and held out her hand again. "Your key. Now."

His smile faded only slightly as he took the key

from his ring and handed it to her. "Okay, but I have a feeling you'll be giving it back before the night is over. I've got the home court advantage here and don't intend to leave without the pennant."

She put the key in the pocket of her jeans. "In addition to being another of your horribly mixed metaphors, that's utterly ridiculous. And you'll be lucky if you leave here with all your teeth." She started to turn away, but he grabbed her around the waist and pulled her against him.

"We'll just see about that."

Jess congratulated herself on the two whole seconds of resistance she managed before kissing him back, but it was little consolation for the repulsion that swept over her moments later when her brain screamed the words that had haunted her for the past few weeks: *Lee's asleep. Who's this?*

She pushed him away and slapped him with all the anger and disgust she felt for him and for herself as well behind the blow. Her vision was so blurred from tears that it was a wonder she didn't miss him, but the pain in her hand when it connected with his face told her she hadn't. She spat on the floor between them and wiped her mouth with the back of her throbbing hand.

"Keep your filthy, cheating mouth away from me, Lee Cassady! You taste like lies and whores, and you make me *sick*."

"Jess, please…" He took a step toward her but stopped when she raised her hand. "I love you."

"Shut up!" She covered her ears and closed her eyes. "I don't want to hear any more of your lies!"

He trapped her inside his arms against the counter. "I'm glad you hit me, Jess. I deserve it, but I swear I'm not lying to you. I love you and just want to come home."

She struggled even though she knew it was useless. He was much too strong, and she had always been so pathetically weak when it came to him. "Let me go," she said without conviction. "I hate you."

"No, you don't." He hugged her with his face in her hair. "You love me, and you know I love you."

"I don't know *anything* anymore. Everything I believed in went to New York and didn't come back." Her voice broke and she sobbed against his chest.

"Cry all you need to, baby." He held her and stroked her hair. "Let it all out so we can talk about it."

When her tears slowed, she looked up at him. "How could you do it, Lee? How could you just throw away our marriage like that?"

"I already told you I didn't know what I was doing. I swear I don't remember leaving the reception or going back to my room or *anything* until I woke up the next morning."

She withdrew from his arms but didn't push him away. "Well, why would you get so drunk in the first place?"

"That's just it. I don't even remember drinking that much."

"What are you trying to say?"

"Let's go sit down so we can talk." He led her into the living room, and they sat on the couch facing each other. "I've been racking my brain trying to figure it all out, and I realized the last thing I can remember clearly is the drink Lynn gave me right after we met at the reception."

Jess scoffed. "Lynn? You mean her name wasn't

Barbie or Bambi?"

He waved away her question. "Think about what I'm saying, Jess. There must've been something in the drink she gave me."

She blinked in surprise. "You think she drugged you?"

"Yeah, I do." He nodded for emphasis. "I even remember the drink tasting funny."

Jess looked skeptical. "She drugged you to get you into bed? You're not *that* good-looking, Lee."

"No, I think she wanted to blackmail me."

"For what—our tax refund? We're not rich."

"No, for a job."

"Oh, give it up." Jess leaned back and folded her arms across her chest. "Nobody would blackmail you for a job with the *Espanola Times* even if you had any hiring authority, which you don't."

"Yeah, but she didn't know I was with the *Espanola Times*." He reached into his pocket for something. "The conference screwed up my name badge. See, it said I was with ESPN."

Jess took the badge from him and read it with hope speeding up her pulse. Her heart wanted desperately to believe him, but her head wasn't ready to concede yet.

"So why are you just realizing all this now? It's a bit too convenient, I think."

"No, it isn't, Jess. I told you from the beginning I couldn't remember what happened. I thought it was just because I must've drank a lot more than I realized, but when I came across the badge in my suitcase this morning, something clicked. I think she used that date rape drug that Fred did the feature on last month. Remember, it was called hip-something."

"Rohypnol," she said. "It's called roofies on the street."

"Yeah, that's it. She must've put one in the drink she gave me, because I don't remember anything after drinking it except waking up in the morning and asking her why the hell she was in my room."

She narrowed her eyes. "Then why hasn't she called here trying to blackmail you?"

"Because I told her I didn't work for ESPN the next morning when she asked me where they were sending me next. She got mad because I didn't tell her sooner and left right after that."

Jess threw the badge at him. "So you knew she thought you were with ESPN and didn't straighten her out right away? Oh, I can just see it. You were too busy playing the big shot to see her put something in your drink—if that's even true."

"Wait, Jess. Listen—"

"Save it, Lee. You've always loved it when women fawn all over you, and since you were mad at me for not going to the conference with you, I'm sure you really egged her on."

"I'll admit I flirt sometimes, but it never goes beyond joking around. You know that, Jess. And you also know the only way I would've ever gone to my room with her was if I didn't know what I was doing because she drugged me."

Jess shook her head. "Even if that's true—and I'm not convinced by any means—it's still your fault this happened. You know you shouldn't have been at the damn conference in the first place."

"No, I know I shouldn't have been at the damn conference *alone*."

"You're unbelievable, Lee. Only someone as selfish as you would expect me to miss my only sister's wedding just to watch you schmooze your way to a better job."

"Selfish? Who the hell do you think I'm doing it for?"

"Not me," she said. "When have I ever complained about how much money you make or where we live? You're the one who's always pining for things we don't need just because they're status symbols."

"Well, excuse me for not being satisfied with middle class life in suburban Georgia and wanting something better." He stuffed the badge into his pocket and leaned back.

Jess stood up then bent over to look him right in the eyes. "You just summed up our biggest problem, Lee. You're not satisfied with anything about your life, including *me*."

"Oh, here we go." He stared at the ceiling and sighed. "This is where you tell me how unappreciated I make you feel and how much I take you for granted."

"Wrong." She walked away so he wouldn't see her angry tears. "This is where I tell you to get out."

"Jess, wait." He followed her into the kitchen. "You know I didn't mean *you* when I said I wanted something better."

"Just go away. Go pursue your dream career without the hindrance of a wife. Screw your way to the big time if that's what it takes."

He caught her arm and turned her around. "I don't want the big time without you. Don't you know that?"

"No, Lee. I don't."

He put his hands on her cheeks and made her look

16

at him. "Jessica Elaine Cassady, I love you and can't make it without you. Please let me come home."

She searched his eyes for sincerity and could see he was truly miserable and afraid of losing her, but she wasn't sure if it was because he loved her or because he depended on her so much for help with his writing.

"Why do you love me, Lee? Give me the right answer and you can come back tonight."

He answered without the slightest hesitation. "I love you because you believed I could make it as a journalist when nobody else did, even me. You made me see there's more to me than meets the eye."

She could tell he thought it was the answer she wanted and didn't have a clue about how disappointing it was to hear that she was only important to him because she helped him feel good about himself. He'd been self-absorbed for as long as she'd known him and she'd let him get away with it until now, but she suddenly decided that being his biggest cheerleader wasn't enough for her anymore. Maybe it was her rapidly approaching thirtieth birthday or the amplified ticking of her biological clock, but she was tired of being Head Groupie on the Lee Cassady Road to Glory Tour.

"You know, Lee, I'm sure those are the reasons you fell for me in the first place, and I guess that's even my fault for the most part, but that shouldn't still be why you love me. After seven years of marriage, if you don't know me well enough to figure out the answer I want to hear—no, that I *deserve* to hear—then I don't think I want to be married to you anymore."

His eyes were a confused blue. "What are you talking about? Just tell me what you want to hear and

I'll say it. Whatever you want."

She laughed without any mirth. "No, this is one thing you'll have to do without any help from me. I'm tired of playing second fiddle to your career and anything else that interests you. If our marriage is as important to you as you claim it is, then you'll make me a priority for once in your life and figure out what I'm talking about."

"That's not fair, Jess. You have to give me something to go on here."

"Don't act as if I haven't told you how I felt dozens of times before." She walked back into the living room and sat on the couch. "Maybe you should have paid attention instead of telling me I was making a big deal out of nothing. Well, it had better be a big deal to you now, Hot Stuff, or I'm going through with the divorce."

He looked pensive a moment and apparently decided it was an improvement over the way things had been when the night began. "Can I at least come home while I'm trying to figure it out?"

"No. We're officially separated until I decide what I need to do."

"So, it's kind of like we're dating again, huh?" He sat beside her and put his arm behind her on the back of the couch. "Yeah, I can go for that. Remember all those weekends of marathon lovemaking when I uncovered the wanted woman inside you?"

She rolled her eyes. "You mean the *wanton* woman? I don't recall being on the run back then."

He snickered. "Oh, you were definitely wanted, baby."

"Well, that's probably what clouded my judgment," she said. "And it's the main reason I don't want you here. I don't plan to make the same mistake again."

"But sometimes even the best laid plans don't succeed, my love." He leaned closer and trailed a fingertip along her collarbone. "You're not fooling me no matter how many times you say you hate me. I felt how much you wanted me when I kissed you, and I know you can't sleep in our bed every night without remembering all the times I've made love to you there. Once I get the chance again to show you how much I love you, I know all the right words will come to me."

Faced with the evocative memories he'd already summoned, the intoxicating effect of his distinctly masculine Lee-scent, and the magnetic pull his body had always had on hers, Jess was acutely reminded of why she'd let him get away with his selfishness for so long.

She struggled to hide her inner chaos and keep her voice steady.

"Sorry, lover boy, but you won't be getting that chance this time. Unless inspiration strikes you some other way, you're going to find yourself a free agent again. Now go away."

She pushed him and got up in what she hoped he would take for disinterest—as if he didn't know he was as tempting to her as a dangling piece of string is to a cat.

True to form, he followed her undaunted to the kitchen and caught her hand.

"Can't I at least stay and have one of the éclairs I bought?"

She looked from the box of pastries to his face, wondering which of them was harder to resist. And which was worse for her.

"Okay, but just one, Lee."

His mouth curved into a maddening smile. "Thanks, baby. I'll have mine for breakfast."

Chapter Three

Jess woke around midnight, breathless from another torrid dream starring Lee and the shameless hussy she turned into whenever she fell asleep. After checking his spot beside her in the bed to make sure she hadn't wimped out and let him stay after all, she got up and went into the bathroom for a drink of water before her mouth developed tumbleweeds. When she returned and saw the hair on the floor beside the bed, her stomach threatened to expel the water she'd just consumed.

Had she really pulled that much hair before she fell asleep? She remembered having a hard time focusing on the book she was reading, but she had no recollection of pulling more than a strand or two. She got a small whisk broom and pan from under the sink in the bathroom to sweep up the hair, and there had to be at least fifty strands.

Remembering one of the tips she'd read online, she searched her closet until she found a pair of evening gloves she'd worn a few years back when she and Lee had attended a Mardi Gras ball with some friends in Mobile. Since she only pulled with her left hand for some reason, she put on the left glove and dropped the right one into the drawer of her night stand. She got back into bed with Ming eyeing her curiously.

"Who are you, the fashion feline?" Jess said. "If

it'll work until my book comes and I can find a better solution, I don't care how ridiculous it looks."

She couldn't go back to sleep, but at least the glove kept her from pulling her hair distractedly while her mind was occupied with more thoughts of Lee. His story about being drugged was definitely suspect, but she knew he wasn't lying when he said his flirting had always been innocent. She didn't really believe he would ever cheat on her. He might be an insensitive, self-centered, materialistic jerk who loved getting attention from women, but he'd never given her any reason to question his fidelity.

The best she could figure—using the vast knowledge of amateur psychology she'd acquired from *Redbook* and *Cosmopolitan*—she thought she must subconsciously want to put the cheating question aside because their other problems bothered her so much more. Like the reason they'd been fighting when he left for the conference. He knew damn well how her mother always made her feel around her beautiful, stylish sister Elise, but the chance to hobnob with the royalty of the sportswriting world—for the second month in a row— had been more important to him than being there for his wife at the wedding.

Jess turned onto her side and scratched Ming between the ears. "Yeah, I knew he was self-absorbed from the beginning, but that doesn't give him *carte blanche* to always put himself first, does it?"

When she and Lee had met as freshmen at Georgia Tech right after his football career ended abruptly with a knee injury, she had shamelessly taken advantage of his need to be validated as something more than an athlete. She'd discovered her intuitive knack for spotting vulnerabilities like that back in high school, and it had never failed to work with the macho types she'd always been attracted to for some mysterious reason.

"I just can't help it." She sighed and moved Ming onto her chest. "I've been addicted to pretty boys ever since I saw the jealousy in Elise's eyes the first time Ricky Castillo came over to see me." Ming's ear twitched in what Jess took as curiosity. "What? I've never told you the story of how I stole the teenaged version of Antonio Banderas from Miss Prom Queen?"

By the time she was a freshman in high school, Jess had stopped trying to keep up with an older sister who so effortlessly followed in their mother's beauty queen footsteps. Unlike her sister Elise, Jess had inherited their father's red hair and Irish features instead of their mother's delicate blonde beauty, and she'd also gotten her father's quirky intellect and love of books instead of her mother's refined tastes and fashion sense. Consequently, Jess had long been aware of her mother's dismay over the difference in her two daughters.

So it had been completely by accident when Jess managed to snag the star pitcher on the JV baseball team. Whether they would admit it or not, every girl in the ninth and tenth grades had been in love with Ricky Castillo's Latin good looks and the impressive way he filled out his baseball uniform. Add to that a quiet, rather brooding demeanor that made him seem deep and mysterious, and even Jess—who had previously been more interested in books than boys—noticed Ricky in the English class they had together. In fact, she had taken to secretly watching him.

One day midway through the first quarter, Jess noticed that Ricky would glance at someone else's book every time the teacher told them to turn somewhere in their textbooks by section heading instead of giving the page number. She also couldn't remember ever seeing him do any work in class. And he had to be in serious trouble if he'd been getting his latest girlfriend to do his work for him, because Cyndi Cooper could have crammed for a month and still not scored her bra size on an IQ test.

That day when class was over, Jess followed Ricky to his locker and told him she would be glad to teach him to read if he was tired of faking it. She handed him her phone number and told him to call her if he didn't want people cheating him someday when he became a pro baseball player. She half expected him to tell her to go to hell, but he took her number with an embarrassed smile.

Jess was no dummy. She knew he probably wouldn't have known she was alive if she hadn't guessed his secret and offered to help, and she also knew his only interest in her was as a tutor. But the prospect of having his undivided attention—along with free rein to gaze at his pretty face while she taught him phonics—was too tempting to resist. She thought it would be an amusing diversion and nothing more, until the first time he came over and she saw the look on her sister's face when she walked into the dining room and saw Ricky and Jess together.

"Oh, I didn't know we had company," Elise said, her tangerine-tipped nails slipping prettily through her blonde hair. "Your name's Ricky, isn't it?"

He looked up and did the customary double take

Elise always elicited from boys. "Yeah, Ricky Castillo. Who are you?"

Jess didn't miss the way Elise's eyebrows went up because he didn't already know whose glorious countenance he beheld. *Everyone* knew Elise Hunter—dance squad captain, class treasurer, and shoo-in for sophomore homecoming maid.

"This is my sister, Elise." Jess couldn't resist adding, "You don't know her, Ricky?"

"No, but there's lots of people I don't know yet. I didn't go to Jackson last year."

Elise was nothing but smiles again. "Oh, that makes sense then."

After giving her one more appreciative glance, Ricky turned back to Jess. "We better get back to...uh, studying. I gotta be home by ten."

"What are you studying?" Elise sat beside him and scooted her chair closer. "Maybe I can help."

He closed the phonics workbook and put it in his lap, then he leaned back and put an arm across Jess's shoulders. "Nah, me and Jess got it covered. Don't we, baby?"

Jess knew exactly what he was doing—pretending to like her so Elise would leave, because he didn't want anyone to know what they were doing. But the only thing Jess cared about at the moment was the spark of jealousy changing her sister's eyes from blue to green, and she fanned it without a trace of remorse.

Giggling for all she was worth, she linked her fingers with Ricky's over her left shoulder and said, "Elise, close the door on your way out, okay?"

Elise stood up, her eyes now a much darker shade of their normal color. "Fine. I have to go call Jeff anyway. Surely you know Jeff Faraway, Ricky. He's on the *varsity* football team."

Ricky snickered. "Yeah, I hit a homerun off him in the Babe Ruth playoffs last summer. Tell him I said better luck with football."

Jess had to bite her lip to keep from laughing when Elise's flawless complexion went from golden to crimson in a matter of seconds. She left the room in a Love's Baby Soft-scented huff and shut the door hard enough to draw a reprimand from their father in the living room.

"Sorry about that." Jess laughed openly once Elise was gone. "I'm sure she won't bother us anymore, but the way she acted makes me think it might be a good idea if you told Cyndi the truth about what we're doing so she won't get the wrong idea."

"Don't worry about that." Ricky shrugged and opened the workbook again. "We broke up last weekend anyway. Let's get back to work."

He made slow but steady progress, and by the time he had to leave, his confidence had increased noticeably. When Jess walked out on the porch with him to say goodbye, he stopped and took her hand before going down the steps.

"Thanks again for doing this. I didn't think it would work, but you make it easy to understand, even for a dumbass like me."

"You're not a dumbass, Ricky. Although it *was* pretty stupid to think you could stay eligible with Cyndi doing your homework." She shoved him playfully.

"Hey, I don't know 'bout that. She manages to pass."

"Yeah, but the men teachers don't give you extra

credit for cleavage."

He laughed and took her other hand. "You're right, and I think it's time I gave smart girls a try anyway. Somebody smart and funny and cute." He moved a step closer to her. "Know anybody like that?"

Jess had always prided herself on being a no-nonsense girl who wasn't afflicted with the boy-craziness most of her friends suffered from. But even though she knew Ricky was only flirting with her out of gratitude or because he thought she might become his new homework supplier, she also knew he was going to kiss her. And she wasn't about to miss out on that opportunity no matter what the motive behind it.

Their tutoring sessions soon became dates, and she was happy when they didn't end as soon as he learned to read. In fact, she was the one who eventually broke up with him because of his unreasonable jealousy and stifling possessiveness.

After their breakup, as is usually the case in the superficial, highly subjective world of high school, Jess discovered that Ricky's popularity and athletic prowess had greatly elevated her own status among her peers. She soon found herself dating quite a few other guys with considerably more brawn than brains, and a big part of their attraction for her was the approval she always saw in her mother's eyes whenever she introduced her latest muscle-bound boyfriend. As far as Jess could remember, it was the only thing she'd ever done that had impressed her mother.

"And Lee was the prettiest pretty boy of them all," Jess said to Ming, although the cat had long since gone to sleep. "Mother practically swooned the first time I took him home to meet her. So, yeah, I know I did all this to myself, but that doesn't mean I have to let it continue, does it? He can either stop being so self-centered or start being single again. Right?" When Ming only purred in response, Jess sighed. "Yeah, I don't expect him back either."

The funny thing was, she had actually thought Lee was different from his predecessors when she'd met him in her freshman journalism class at Georgia Tech. She had noticed him immediately, of course, but she didn't actually meet him until he came back to class after his knee surgery and she offered to help him catch up on the work he'd missed. The first time they met at the library, she had commented on a letter to his parents that she noticed on the first page of his notebook.

"I write to them every week," he said without a trace of self-consciousness. "And I call home every Sunday when the rates go down."

"You must be really close to them," Jess said. "I think that's great. I wish I were closer to my family."

"Yeah, we're pretty tight. My dad's the greatest guy I've ever known, and my mom and my little sister think I came here from the planet Krypton."

Jess laughed. "Were they at the game when you hurt your knee?"

His face sobered. "No, my dad had to work that weekend, thank God. They know I got hurt, but they don't know how bad it is. I don't know how I'm gonna tell them the truth—that I can't play anymore. Football's the only thing I can do."

Jess didn't know him well enough to disagree, but her intuition told her there was more to him than just a pretty face and divine muscles.

"Then why are in a journalism class?" she said.

"Have you done any writing before?"

He shrugged. "I wrote a few sports articles for the school newspaper in high school. My friends liked them, and my English teacher said they were decent. Since I had to choose a major for college, I picked journalism, but I never really expected to do anything but play football. I should probably just go back home and get a job at the power plant where my dad works." He slapped the notebook shut and looked at his bandaged knee in disgust.

"Well, you should at least get an unbiased opinion of your writing before you give up," she said. "Do you have any samples I can read?"

He looked at her intently. "Yeah, but you don't have to do that."

"I don't mind, really. But I should warn you that I'm extremely critical and brutally honest when it comes to writing."

He pretended to chew his fingernails. "I don't know if I've got the guts for something like that. You're pretty scary."

She nodded with a wry smile. "Yeah, I always heard baseball players are a lot tougher than football players. I guess it's true."

"Baseball players can kiss my ass." He scoffed and reached into his bag to take out another notebook. "Here's a story I wrote about the state championship game we played my senior year. Do your worst, scary lady."

She read it with her eyes gradually widening in surprise at how good it was. His mechanics were weak, but he had an unpretentious style and an engaging voice filled with genuine emotion that came through clearly in his words. Jess was truly impressed. And when she looked up and saw how anxiously he'd been awaiting her appraisal, she knew the story she held in her hands was much more than just words he'd thrown together on a whimsy. She was holding the key to this particular pretty boy's heart, and she decided to open it and see what was inside.

"Lee, I don't even like football, but this story made me feel all the excitement and emotion you must have felt after winning the championship game. You're a natural writer in the rawest of states, and if I ever hear you say anything again about quitting and going home, I'll kick you in your other knee."

His face was transformed by the most dazzling smile she had ever seen. Before she realized what he meant to do, he grabbed her by the shoulders and kissed her. Now, by that time in her life, Jess had kissed plenty of boys—a few had even been somewhat of a local legend because of their aptitude in the lip-lock department—but never had she felt anything like the sensory tsunami that came with Lee's kiss.

And before that first kiss ended, Jess had decided she didn't want to simply look inside this pretty boy's heart. She wanted it to be her home for the rest of her life.

****

She woke in the morning to find she'd taken off the glove sometime during the night, but at least she didn't see any hair on the floor or her pillow. She certainly couldn't wear the glove in public, but maybe it would help when she was home.

She had an éclair with her coffee and couldn't help smiling at the memory of how crestfallen Lee had been when he'd realized she really meant it and wasn't letting him stay. The concept of any woman being able to resist him when he was trying so hard to be charming was something his conceited little brain just couldn't process.

The phone rang as she poured her second cup of coffee, so she answered it with, "No, I didn't take him back."

"What happened?" Deb demanded.

"He claims he was drugged by an ambitious bimbo who thought he worked for ESPN."

"Uh-huh. And did he provide you with hip waders before shoveling that story?"

Jess laughed. "No, but he did bring me éclairs."

"Oh, jeez. All he did was ply you with pastries to get you to swallow that hogwash? You could've at least held out for jewelry."

"I didn't say I believed him, although he could very well be telling the truth. The conference put ESPN on his ID badge by mistake. He showed it to me."

Deb still sounded unconvinced. "And why was he accepting drinks from bimbos in the first place? Did you ask him *that*?"

"Yes, Deb, and I also told him we have much bigger problems that have nothing to do with drugs *or* bimbos, such as his love affair with himself and his complete disregard for my feelings."

"Well, that's more like it," Deb said. "So when's the appointment with your lawyer?"

"I haven't actually talked to one yet."

"Jessica Elaine Cassady!"

"Don't call me that, Deb. You sound like my mother, and that's *not* a good thing."

"Speaking of Mommie Dearest, what does she have to say about all this?"

Jess sank into a chair as her mother's presence descended on her with its customary oppression. "She doesn't know, and I don't intend to tell her. And if you're thinking of ratting me out, you should know that she won't be on your side."

"You think she'd want you to take him back?"

"I don't think, I know. She'll assume it's all my fault and tell me to stop being so 'inflexible.' As far as she's concerned, Lee is the only thing about me she has to be proud of. I'm sure she wouldn't want to lose him."

Deb sighed. "Did she give you a hard time at the wedding?"

"You mean when she could take a break from playing the Queen Mother who had to be consulted about every aspect of the elaborate wedding she finally got to have, thanks to her only *considerate* daughter. How selfish of me to have a simple wedding, you know."

"Did she ask why Lee wasn't with you?"

"Of course. I told her the paper sent him to another convention. I guess she was too busy giving orders to dig any deeper. Fortunately, I escaped before she had a chance to regroup after Elise and Garrett left on their cruise."

Deb's tone softened. "Want me to come over or meet you somewhere for lunch? We can go shopping afterward and spend all Lee's money."

"No, I think I'll stay home and get some things done. Besides, I'm hoping my book comes today, and I want to read it as soon as it gets here."

"Jess, alphabetizing your CDs is no way to spend a Saturday. Let's go have some fun."

"Ha, lot you know. I did that last weekend. Today I'm organizing my bookshelves by genre." Jess paused to laugh. "But if it makes you feel any better, it'll drive Lee crazy when he sees it."

Deb snickered. "In that case, I'll come help you."

Jess checked her e-mail after she hung up and found a message from Lee telling her to save the last éclair so they could share it in bed the next time he came over—and would tonight be okay? She sent a reply saying he still didn't get it and wouldn't be getting any until he did, so he'd be wise to spend the evening in deep thought.

As if that was likely to happen. She knew he'd been staying with his friend Trent because he didn't want his mother or sister to know he'd been thrown out, and Jess didn't want them to find out either. Even at her anger's zenith right after he came back from New York, she'd never really considered telling them. Ever since his father's sudden death from a heart attack two years ago, Lee's mother and sister had depended heavily on him, and Jess couldn't bring herself to tarnish him in their eyes no matter how furious she was. She'd always been proud of him for his devotion to his family and wasn't sure she would ever get over the loyalty she felt to him when it came to things like that.

When the doorbell rang a little later while she was taking all her books off the shelves, she expected it to be either Lee or Deb, so she opened it wearing a sardonic smile that disappeared the instant she saw her mother's face.

Chapter Four

"Hello, Jessica." Marjorie Hunter's cultured Southern drawl sent Ming into hiding behind the sofa. "A delivery truck was here when I drove up, so I signed for this package. It appears to be a book."

Jess took the package and put it on the foyer table. "What are you doing here, Mother? Is something wrong? Where's Daddy?"

"My, what a warm greeting." Marjorie came in and set down her bag. "Must there be something wrong for me to visit, and am I only welcome if I bring your father with me?"

"No, of course not." Jess forced a smile as Marjorie hugged her. "I just wasn't expecting you."

"Put my bag in the guest room and go make us some coffee, dear. I didn't get my usual two cups this morning and couldn't bring myself to drink that dreadful brew they sell on the road." Marjorie paused at the entrance to the living room and turned to look at Jess again. "Where's my handsome son-in-law?"

Jess picked up her mother's bag and avoided her gaze. "He's not here right now. I'm not sure when he'll be back."

"Where is he?"

Jess tried to squeeze past her mother and escape down the hall to the guest bedroom, but Marjorie caught her arm. "Jessica, I asked you a question.

Where's Lee?"

Jess's stomach knotted the way it always did when she was about to get one of her mother's patented lectures, and she realized her hand was in her hair. She stuffed it in her pocket and decided she couldn't deal with her mother's criticism right now on top of everything else.

"He's…playing handball with his friend Trent."

Marjorie's steel-gray eyes narrowed, and Jess knew she hadn't missed the hesitation in her hastily concocted reply. She was probably there because she'd suspected something at the wedding after all, and Jess knew she wouldn't leave until she found out everything she wanted to know. As much as she hated to do it, she'd have to call Lee and get him to come home until her mother left.

"How long will you be staying?"

"Is there a problem with my being here, Jessica? You seem exceptionally eager to be rid of me."

Jess shook her head and walked toward the extra bedroom. "Don't be silly, Mother. I'm happy to see you, it's just unexpected. I may need to adjust our plans for the weekend."

"No need to cancel anything on my account." Marjorie followed Jess down the hall. "I certainly don't need you and Lee to babysit me. I just came to spend some time with my daughter and talk."

Jess's mental copyeditor thought *pry* would have been a more accurate verb choice.

"There's nothing to cancel." Jess put the suitcase on the bed. "I'm just trying to get an agenda for the next few days. You know how I am about organization."

"Ah, yes, organization," Marjorie said from the doorway. "One of the euphemisms for the peculiar obsessions you inherited from your father and also one of the reasons I left him at home. Don't frown that way, Jessica. You'll get a permanent crease in your forehead."

Jess stuffed her hand deeper into her pocket as she followed her mother back to the living room. "How long did you say you could stay?"

"I didn't, and it depends." Marjorie sat on the couch and patted her perfect champagne-blonde curls. "Hurry and go put on the coffee, dear. I don't want a headache while we have our chat."

When the coffee was ready, Jess went to summon Marjorie from the snooping she was undoubtedly doing in the living room and was horrified to see her mother had opened the package she'd brought in and was flipping through the pages of the book with a horrified expression of her own.

"Why in Heaven's name did you order this book, Jessica?"

Jess snatched it in exasperation. "Opening someone else's mail is a federal offense, Mother."

"Then you may call the FBI after you answer my question. What is this hair-pulling nonsense about?"

"It's not nonsense. It's a biological condition that makes people pull their hair to restore balance in their nervous systems." Jess paused to muster her courage. "It's called trichotillomania, and I have it."

"You have no such thing. Where did you get a ridiculous idea like that?"

"I researched it on the Internet, and it's not ridiculous." Jess set her jaw in what she hoped resembled defiance. "You've noticed it yourself, Mother. How many times did you tell me to leave my hair alone while I was home for the wedding?"

"Yes, you've always had a bothersome habit of playing with your hair, but that doesn't mean you have this…trichopullomania nonsense. I've heard about those people. They pull out their hair by the handfuls and chew on it or something equally repulsive. I refuse to believe any daughter of *mine* does anything so revolting."

Jess's brave façade crumbled in the face of her mother's disgust, and she lowered her gaze to the book in her hands. Why couldn't it have arrived just one day earlier?

"It's tricho*till*omania, Mother. It's derived from the Greek words for—"

"Jessica Elaine Hunter, don't you dare try to skirt the issue with me! There's nothing wrong with you except the inability to control your bad habits. What does your husband have to say about all this?"

"He doesn't pay enough attention to me to even notice!" The words were out of Jess's mouth before she could stop them.

Marjorie folded her arms in front of her. "Where is Lee really? I knew there was more to his absence than just work when he wasn't with you at the wedding. What have you done, Jessica?"

Jess sat on the couch with the book on her lap, fighting her angry tears. "Why do you automatically assume *I* did something? Why wouldn't you be on my side, at least to begin with?"

"I'm not on anyone's side," Marjorie said. "I just want you to tell me what's going on, and I expect an answer this instant."

The phone rang and Jess practically sprinted down the hall to answer the extension in the bedroom, grateful for the reprieve. Maybe it was because he'd rescued her for the moment, but when she heard Lee's voice, she felt an inexplicable wave of affection for him and might have hugged him if he'd been there in person.

"I'm glad you called, Lee. My mother showed up here uninvited, and I don't want her to know we're separated. I need you to come home and stay until she's gone."

"Well, hot damn," he said. "If it means I get to come home, I'll be happy to see the snooty old battleaxe."

Jess covered her mouth to keep from laughing. Lee knew her mother too well.

"It's only for a couple of nights," she said, "so just bring your things in a gym bag. And you need to look as if you've been playing handball with Trent all morning."

"Sure, no problem. When should I get there?"

"As soon as you can. I'll tell her you're coming home early to take us to dinner. At least I won't have to cook that way."

"You got it, babe. I was calling to ask you to dinner anyway."

"Okay, I'll see you in a little while." She hesitated before adding, "Thanks for helping, Lee."

"You don't have to thank me, you dope. I love you, Jess."

She hung up and took a quick look in the mirror so she could remember what a full head of hair looked like in case she was bald when the night was over.

She found her mother at the kitchen table with a cup of coffee and the last éclair. "That was Lee. He'll be home in a little while and wants to take us to dinner."

"Wonderful," Marjorie said. "I'm looking forward to seeing him."

Jess poured herself a cup of coffee and sat down across from her mother. "I'll admit Lee and I have argued about his lack of attention to anything but work lately, but that's between the two of us, Mother. I'd appreciate it if you wouldn't mention what I said about him earlier."

Marjorie arched one carefully drawn eyebrow. "I don't need a course in discretion from you, Jessica. I have no intention of repeating your petulant little outburst. However, I do intend to enlist Lee's help in making you see how ludicrous this hair-pulling business is."

"Mother—"

"Don't bother arguing with me. I'm your mother and know what's best. Lee has always been more practical than you, and I'm sure he'll see to it that you break this dreadful habit."

Jess rolled her eyes. "Oh, yes. He's *so* practical. His prescription for every ailment is a backrub and sex."

Marjorie looked aghast. "Well, I certainly didn't need to know *that*."

Jess sipped her coffee to hide a gratified smile. "Sorry, Mother, but this is my problem and I wish you'd let me handle it. I'm an intelligent woman who isn't exactly prone to foolish undertakings, you know."

Marjorie sighed. "Yes, and sometimes I think intelligence is your biggest problem. You overanalyze things and tend to miss the obvious. You simply have a bad habit and need to exercise more self-control."

Jess closed her eyes and reminded herself that this woman had given her life.

"We need to change the subject before I have another petulant outburst, Mother."

"Fine," Marjorie said. "Let's talk about when you plan to give me a grandchild."

By the time Lee arrived, Jess was so desperate to escape from under her mother's microscope that she greeted him with genuine joy and indulged her earlier impulse to hug him.

"Happy to see me, my love?" He laughed softly as he brushed his lips across her cheek.

"Save me," she whispered.

Lee turned to smile at her mother. "Marjorie, you look younger every time I see you. I'm surprised Bill ever lets you out of his sight."

"You're as charmingly dishonest as ever, Lee." Marjorie gave him a much warmer hug than she'd given her daughter. "And Jessica is the one who needs to keep her spouse under close observation. You're much too handsome for your own good."

"Yes, he's a victim of his male pulchritude," Jess said. "We're trying to locate a support group for him."

Marjorie ignored Jess's remark and continued to smile at Lee. "We missed you at the wedding, dear. Elise was a vision as always, but I certainly could've used a handsome escort."

Jess carried the empty coffee cups to the sink. "I'm surprised that pretentious wedding planner didn't provide one for you, Mother. Must've been a headset malfunction."

"I'll have you know Amelia was a *godsend*," Marjorie said. "She made sure all my instructions were carried out to the letter, and she was invaluable in making your sister's wedding the event of the season in Tampa. Everyone says so."

"Of course they do." Jess dried her hands more vigorously than was necessary. "Elise has never failed to make you proud. Has she, Mother?"

Lee evidently recognized the volatile nature of the subject matter, because he said, "Time enough for chitchat at dinner, ladies. We have reservations at Giovanni's for six o'clock."

Marjorie linked her arm with his. "How thoughtful of you, dear. Garrett certainly has his work cut out for him if he wants to become my favorite son-in-law."

"Glad to hear it." Lee winked at Jess as he guided Marjorie from the room. "I may need an ally if my wife ever decides to trade me in for a newer model."

Jess puttered around the kitchen as long as possible before trying to slip past Lee and her mother in the living room, but Marjorie spotted her.

"I told you Lee would agree with me about this hair-pulling nonsense, Jessica. And he most certainly *has* noticed."

Jess frowned at the two of them seated next to each other on the couch, the crease between her brows deepening at the amused expression on her husband's face. "Is there something you find funny about all this, Lee?"

He stood up. "Oh, don't get your bloomers in a bundle. I've known you were hair-obsessed for years."

She continued to frown at him. "You don't know what you're talking about."

"Oh, yes I do." He picked up his bag and took her hand, pulling her toward the bedroom. "Come on and we'll talk about it. Excuse us please, Marjorie."

"Certainly, dear." She gave Jess a self-satisfied smile. "I think I'll go lie down awhile anyway. I don't want a headache to spoil our dinner."

Jess followed Lee to the bedroom, but as soon as the door closed, she snatched her hand from his. "I don't know what you're trying to pull, but you can forget it."

He put his bag on the bed and unzipped it. "Hey, I got your mother to leave you alone, didn't I?"

She narrowed her eyes. "You don't have any idea what she was talking about, do you?"

He shrugged. "I know you always have at least fifty-two bottles of hair products on the shelf in the shower. And I can also remember several times I've had to take your brush away from you so you wouldn't throw it at the mirror when your hair wouldn't do exactly what you wanted. Like I said, you're hair-obsessed. So what?"

"I should've known." Jess sat on the bed and picked up the book she'd ordered. "You never notice anything unless it has something to do with you."

"Oh, quit pouting. I know you play with your hair all the time. I just don't see what's the big deal." He pulled his shirt over his head and sat on the end of the bed. "And even if you think it's more than just a habit, I still don't see the problem. Knowing you, you'll be an expert on the subject in a week and giving lessons on how to control it."

She had to smile at his assumption of her competence. He liked to pick at her about her persnickety ways and nerdy interests, but she'd never really minded his teasing. He'd told her once that she was the smartest girl he'd ever dated so he deserved bonus points on his IQ for getting her to marry him.

She indulged herself in an appreciative survey of the muscles in his back and shoulders while he bent to take off his shoes, loving the way they rippled every time he moved. The immediate rise in her body temperature reminded her of just *how* he'd gotten her to marry him and also of how long she'd been without him. When he stood up suddenly and dropped his shorts, her heart nearly dropped into her stomach.

"What do you think you're doing, Lee? Put your clothes back on!"

He turned around and gave her a bemused look. "I'm gonna take a shower. What's wrong?"

"Nothing." She averted her gaze and flicked her hand at him. "Go in the bathroom, and make sure you get dressed before you come back."

He took her hand and tried to pull her to her feet. "Come with me, Jess. We used to shower together all the time, remember?"

"No. Forget it." She snatched her hand from his, hoping he wouldn't notice how sweaty it was. "I don't shower with men who cheat on me."

"I didn't cheat on you, I was drugged. And since I was passed out the whole time, I don't even think anything happened."

"Nice try, but some parts of you are fully functional in your sleep."

He laughed and sat beside her on the bed. "That's

only when I'm sleeping with you, Jess."

He put his arm around her and nuzzled her neck, escalating her body temperature a few more degrees. She knew she needed to put some distance between them before he made her forget everything except the feel of his lips on her skin and how much she wanted him, but for a few seconds all she could do was surrender to the heat he'd always ignited in her. When his lips drifted to her collarbone and one of his hands slipped under her shirt, she forced herself to push him away and stood up, but he pulled her back down and covered her body with his.

"Lee, stop it." She turned her head to avoid his mouth. "This is why I didn't want you here."

"But you do want me, don't you, baby?" His hand slid inside her shirt and caressed her ribcage and the underside of her breast. "I know everything you want. And I'm the only one who can give it to you."

His arrogant claims during lovemaking had always excited her more, because everything he said was true.

"Lee, please…" She put her hands on his chest and pushed, but the feel of his pectorals beneath her fingers only helped his case. "This doesn't solve anything."

"Yes it does." He lowered his lips to her neck again. "It's been so long, Jess. Can't you tell I'm in agony?"

As much as she wanted him, she knew that if she gave in and let him make love to her, she'd end up letting him come back home and he'd never take her seriously about anything. With a Herculean effort, she pushed him away and twisted one of his nipples.

"There's some real agony for you."

"Ow! Damn, Jess. That hurt." He rolled over and

rubbed his chest. "What'd you do that for?"

"I told you to stop and I meant it. Try that again and you're gone. I'd rather listen to my mother's lectures than let you manipulate me." She picked up her book and started flipping through it.

"Oh, sorry. I forgot you're still pretending to hate me." He sighed and walked toward the bathroom. "Hey, maybe you'll get lucky and I'll slip on the soap in the shower. I'm sure you'd make a lovely widow."

She didn't look up from her book. "Don't get blood on my new shower curtain."

Chapter Five

Throughout dinner, Lee managed to keep Marjorie's attention on subjects other than Jess's hair. In fact, she didn't bring it up again until dessert arrived, making Jess lament the heavenly tiramisu that she wouldn't get to enjoy.

"I certainly hope Lee has put an end to this foolishness about pulling your hair, Jessica." Marjorie tasted her zabaglione custard with an ecstatic roll of her eyes.

"We had a long talk about it," Jess said. "You don't need to worry about it anymore."

Marjorie looked unconvinced. "Humor me with a few details, dear."

"Now, Marjorie." Lee filled her wine glass with Moscato d'Asti. "Didn't I promise I'd take care of it? Jess and I see eye to eye on the subject now. Don't we, love?"

Jess gave him a grateful look. "Yes, we do."

Lee covered Marjorie's hand with his. "See? No need to worry about Jess as long as I'm around. She may not always realize it, but she's my number one priority."

He continued to smile as he looked at Jess, but his eyes had a serious cast that made her heart skip a beat. Maybe he was finally getting a clue after all.

Marjorie sipped her wine with a euphoric sigh.

"Your husband is a treasure, Jessica. I hope you appreciate him."

Jess held out her own glass to Lee. "Well, I do tonight."

She watched him work her mother effortlessly and thought about how his charisma was as much a part of him as his talents for writing and football. Maybe she was being too hard on him. He couldn't help it if women were drawn to him like sugar ants to a piece of candy. He'd said she was his number one priority, hadn't he? Maybe she should just believe it and stop looking for reasons to doubt him.

By the time they got home from the restaurant, Marjorie was so sated with the combination of wine and masculine charm that she kissed Jess goodnight, told her not to worry about anything, and floated off to bed humming "Volaré." Jess went to find Lee so she could thank him and found him in the bedroom unpacking his bag.

"I only brought enough clothes for the weekend," he said, "but I can pick up some more tomorrow if you think your mother will be staying longer."

"Maybe you should bring all your things home, Lee."

He looked up and dropped the bag to go to her. "You won't be sorry. I promise."

She closed her eyes and leaned against him as he put his arms around her. "Swear you'll never do anything like this again. Make me believe you so I can forget that phone call that made me want to die."

"Jess, baby." He tilted up her face and brushed her tears away with his thumbs. "I'm so sorry I hurt you, and I swear—"

The phone rang and he stopped talking so he could turn to look at it. A red number *2* was blinking on the message display.

"Hold on a second, baby. I need to answer that." He picked up the receiver and sat on the side of the bed.

Utterly stupefied, Jess's mouth fell open as she listened to him tell Trent that no, he hadn't had a chance to listen to the messages yet.

"Thanks, man," he said after listening a few seconds. "I owe you one for this." He hung up and immediately pressed the replay button on the answering machine.

"Lee, what the hell are you doing?" Jess said when she finally regained the ability to speak. "That can wait until later."

He held up his hand to silence her as the message played, and she had to fight the urge to take off one of her shoes and throw it at his head. When an unfamiliar woman's voice spoke on the tape, blood rushed to Jess's face before it all plummeted to her feet.

"*Good evening, Lee. This is Cassandra Wilhelm with* Sports Spotlight. *I so enjoyed our phone conversation the other night and was hoping we could get together while I'm in Atlanta so we can talk further about your working for us. Give me a call at the mobile number on the card I gave you in New York, and we'll have lunch one day next week if you're free. I'm really looking forward to seeing you again and hearing all about your talents in that delightful Southern accent of yours. Ciao.*"

Lee jumped up and turned to Jess as if he expected her to be excited. "Did you hear that, baby? *Sports Spotlight*, the top sports magazine in the world!"

"Yes, I heard. And I'm *so* glad you'll have something to keep you busy after the divorce!" She picked up his bag and threw it at him. "Get out! I'll tell my mother the truth in the morning. I'd rather listen to her lecture than look at your selfish face another second!"

"Wait, let me explain." He tossed the bag aside and moved toward her, but she backed away as if he were contagious with the Black Death.

"Don't you dare touch me. I don't want to hear anything you have to say! You had your chance to talk and stopped to take your damn phone call!"

"But, Jess—"

"Don't even try to justify yourself, Lee! If you can't even put aside your precious career goals long enough to apologize for hurting me, then I don't want to hear anything else you have to say. Actually, I'm glad this happened. At least it kept me from falling for your lies again!"

"Just let me tell you what that was—"

"Get *out*! Get out or I'll call your mother and tell her what a liar you are!"

He winced, and she almost told him she didn't mean it. Fool that she was, she might be mad enough to murder him, but she'd never hurt him like that. She'd have to be sure and laugh at the irony some other time.

"Okay," he said. "I'll go if that's what you want, but you're wrong. I know you don't think you ever make a mistake, but you're sure as hell making one now."

He grabbed his bag and walked to the door. Ming tried to run in when he opened it, and he pushed her aside with his foot as he left. Jess picked up the offended cat and buried her face in the fur on the back of her neck.

"It's okay, girl. He's gone for good this time."

****

In the morning, Jess considered making up something to tell her mother that would explain Lee's absence, but since she'd decided to go through with the divorce and would have to tell her parents eventually, she might as well face the music now and get it over with. When Marjorie entered the kitchen at seven, Jess had a western omelet waiting for her.

"Thank you, dear," Marjorie said as she sat down. "But you shouldn't have gone to so much trouble."

Jess set a cup of coffee in front of her mother and went back to pour one for herself. "It was no trouble, Mother. I know how much you love them."

Marjorie took a bite and chewed with her eyes closed. "It's delicious. No one makes these as well as you and your father."

Jess sat across from her at the table and traced the pattern on the cup with her thumb. "I'm glad you like it."

"Aren't you eating, dear?"

"No, I had a granola bar earlier. I'm not really a breakfast person."

"Well, Lee certainly is." Marjorie put down her fork and took a sip of coffee. "Isn't he joining us?"

Jess took a fortifying breath. "Lee isn't here. He's been staying with his friend Trent since right after Elise's wedding because we're getting a divorce." She looked up and met her mother's accusing gaze as steadily as she could manage.

Marjorie set down her cup and pushed away her

plate. "Then perhaps you wouldn't mind explaining that little tableau the two of you performed last night."

"I'm sorry, Mother. I should have told you the truth as soon as you arrived. I thought for a while last night that we might work things out and there would be nothing to tell, but I was wrong."

"Well, go on, Jessica. Tell me why your husband left you."

Jess's outrage presented itself in a bitter laugh that burst from her mouth with such force that it caused her to spill some of her coffee. When her mother's face turned an unflattering shade of magenta in response, Jess almost laughed again with genuine mirth.

"I fail to see anything remotely humorous about this, Jessica Elaine. Have you taken leave of your senses?"

"Yes, that's it, Mother." Jess took a napkin from the apple-shaped holder in the center of the table and blotted the spilled coffee. "Lee left me because I'm insane. He's probably afraid I'll murder him in his sleep or—even worse—that I might pull out *his* hair and make everyone think he has male pattern baldness."

Marjorie folded her arms across her chest. "I didn't realize you were such a comedienne, dear. You've obviously been wasting your talent at that newspaper."

Jess smiled. "Good one, Mother. I guess I got my talent for sarcasm from you."

Marjorie still looked as though she were still trying to decide whether or not to call the men with the nets. "Stop all this nonsense and answer my question. Why did Lee move out?"

"Because I threw him out!" Jess stood up and slapped the table with her palms. "A woman answered the phone in his hotel room in the middle of the night, so I threw all his clothes into the front yard and told him I wanted a divorce. And although I'm sure you'll still find some way to make this my fault, your favorite son-in-law is the one who screwed up!"

Marjorie looked surprised, but her expression quickly changed to one of doubt. "Well, I'm sure there's a reasonable explanation. Did you give him a chance to explain?"

"Yes, and I'm not letting him smooth-talk his way out of this."

"What did he say?"

Jess wiped up the rest of the spilled coffee and took her cup to the sink in exasperation. "That doesn't matter. Even if I believed him, it wouldn't change anything because this isn't the only problem we have. It just highlighted the others and brought everything to a head. He had no business being in New York in the first place because he should have been at Elise's wedding with me."

Marjorie's tone remained unsympathetic. "Well, since he came back last night to help you dupe me, he's obviously trying to make amends. It seems to me you've made your point. You'll only be cutting off your nose to spite your face if you persist with a divorce out of stubbornness or wounded pride. You can't afford to let a man like Lee get away, Jessica."

Jess whirled around to face her. "And what kind of a man would that be? The kind that deserts his wife so he can run off to New York for the third time in two months and do God knows what to get himself a better job? Or do you mean the kind that did me such a favor by marrying me in the first place when we both know he could've had someone beautiful and sophisticated like Elise? Which kind of man do you mean, Mother?"

"Leave your sister and your jealousy out of this, Jessica. We're talking about your marriage."

"I'm not *jealous* of Elise. I've just always wondered why you so obviously think beauty and fashion sense are more important than intelligence and talent."

"That's ridiculous, and you're only trying to change the subject." Marjorie got up to refill her coffee cup. "Lee is an extremely handsome man, so I think it's actually quite remarkable for this to be the first time in seven years of marriage that anything like this has happened. You should be glad he's asked you to forgive him and wants to come back to you."

"Mother, you can't be serious," Jess said. "Are you trying to tell me you'd be willing to just forgive and forget if Daddy did something like this?"

"Yes, that's exactly what I'm saying. Men are plagued by dreadfully bothersome libidos and can't be faulted for their primitive needs." Marjorie's posture reflected her supercilious tone. "As long as they're discreet and sufficiently penitent, I tend to see it as a welcome reprieve."

Jess's anger receded in the face of her mother's confession. She'd never thought of her parents as an overly happy couple, but she'd had no idea until now of how little affection there was between them. She knew her mother considered sex a distasteful subject, and now she realized Marjorie felt the same way about the act itself. For the first time in her life, Jess actually felt sorry for her mother.

"Well, I'm afraid I don't see it that way. I'm

calling a lawyer tomorrow."

"You're making a grave mistake, Jessica. Your husband will be snatched up by some opportunistic woman, and you'll end up with no one but your cat for companionship."

"Then maybe I'll get a whole house full," Jess said. "Start saving cat food coupons for me, Mother."

Chapter Six

Jess saw a lawyer the next day and started divorce proceedings. Lee didn't attempt to dissuade her with notes and gifts as he'd been doing for the past week, so she took it to mean he'd decided that a divorce was for the best. She realized she was wrong a few days later when he threw the papers on her desk at work.

"I'm not signing these," he said. "Maybe I don't know how to change your mind or make you see what a big mistake you're making, but I'm sure as hell not gonna go along with it. Consider your damn divorce contested, Mrs. Cassady."

Jess tossed the papers back at him. "It won't do you any good, Lee. All you're doing is wasting your time and your money."

He leaned over and dropped the papers into the waste basket beside her desk. "Well, the way I see it, my love, I have nothing to lose. I've got plenty of free time now, and the more money I spend fighting your stupid divorce, the less there'll be for you to take."

When Jess told Deb at lunch that Lee had refused to sign the papers, she was surprised at Deb's reaction.

"He must think he can change your mind," she said as she shook a copious amount of Tabasco sauce onto her enchiladas. "At least he doesn't give up easily. I'll grant him that."

Jess lowered her forkful of chimichanga and

scowled at Deb's lack of venom. "Jeez, that was almost a compliment. What happened to your campaign to get him tarred and feathered?"

Deb shrugged. "Howie thinks I pushed you into this, and I'm kinda afraid he's right. Don't get me wrong, you know I've never liked the way Lee takes you for granted, and it really burns my butt the way he takes all the credit for his articles when we both know they'd be incomprehensible without your input. But regardless of how I feel about the jerk, I don't want you doing something as permanent as a divorce unless you're positive it's what you really want."

"Don't worry, I'm positive." Jess sat up a little taller and squared her shoulders. "Like I told my mother, I refuse to be browbeaten or taken for granted by anyone from now on. I intend to focus on me and what I need for a change."

"I'm sure that went over with her like a lead balloon," Deb said. "But good for you."

Driving home after work, Jess thought about her show of bravado with Deb and wished she felt half as confident and decisive as she sounded. But at least now she had plenty of free time to do some research on trichotillomania—or TTM as it was called for short.

The book she'd ordered had turned out to be a goldmine of information on the underlying causes, identification methods and treatment options. Self-acceptance and learning to refocus emotional energies were key elements in the treatment plan, so she began meditating twice a day to help center herself. Not only did she enjoy it, she was amazed at how it allowed her to see all the parallels between hair pulling and other aspects of her life. Armed with as much knowledge about TTM as possible, Jess knew she could handle it, just as she was handling her transition to becoming an unattached, independent woman for the first time in her life. Except for the two months she'd lived in the dorm at Georgia Tech before she met Lee, she had never lived on her own. Now that she and Ming had the house all to themselves, it was nice having no one to answer to.

In addition to little things like cooking only when she felt like it and being able to play her Michael Bublé CDs as loud as she wanted without always having to compete with *Sports Center* on television, Jess took advantage of her freedom and indulged herself in a little pampering. She signed up for yoga classes, had her first pedicure, took lessons in the Japanese art of Sumi-e, and began attending a lecture series on the Revolutionary War—a subject that had always fascinated her. Deb told her nobody but the heroine in the nerdiest chick lit novel ever written would call any of those things pampering, but Jess was having too much fun to care.

In fact, she was enjoying herself so much that the only time she missed Lee was when she saw him at work—more irony she'd have to laugh at someday. And although he'd followed through on his promise to contest the divorce, Jess thought he seemed pretty damn unconcerned about their separation. Knowing Lee, she figured he must think she couldn't possibly want any man but him and wasn't worried about what she was doing while they were apart.

It almost seemed as if he were avoiding her, so it was only by accident that she overheard two of the other sportswriters in the break room talking about

Lee's upcoming interview in New York with the editors of *Sports Spotlight*. Evidently, he'd used his "delightful Southern accent" to charm the woman who'd left him the message.

When she got back to her desk, Jess called his extension to see if his new employment opportunity meant he would tell his lawyer to stop inventing roadblocks to stall the divorce.

"Not a chance, Mrs. Cassady," he said. "In fact, my lawyer says this will give us even more levitation for delays."

Jess rolled her eyes. "You mean leverage, Lee? Or has your head swelled so much you've begun to float?"

"Leverage—right. See how much I need you?"

"Yeah, well, your new employer can hire you a personal editor, because I've officially resigned from the position. You've got what you've always wanted, so why don't you go enjoy it and leave me alone?"

He sighed. "For someone who thinks she knows it all, you sure don't know much about me. When have I ever conceded in any game?"

"You think of our marriage as a game? That's so typical." She started to hang up then added, "Feel free to hit the bimbo circuit while you're in New York. Maybe one of them will do me a favor and take you off my hands."

"No can do, baby, but thanks for calling to wish me luck. I'll bring you back a postcard from Rockefeller Center."

Jess treated herself to another pedicure on her way home from work and decided to show it off that night by wearing her new sandals to the second installment of her lecture series. As she drove to Hayden Junior

College, she couldn't help smiling as she admired the "Prom Night" polish on her perfectly tapered toes. It was silly and she wouldn't dream of admitting it to anyone, but she'd always been proud of her feet and secretly loved it whenever someone complimented them. And Lee had told her once that her feet were a lot prettier than the ones in magazine ads, and he liked to joke about how he wanted her to become a famous foot model so he could buy a Maserati and be a kept man.

Her pedicure lost all its capacity for cheering her up as she remembered the day in their sophomore year of college when she and Lee had both cut class to spend the afternoon together and he'd made up a silly poem titled "Ode to Jess's Toes" that he'd recited for her on his knees. She'd laughed until she cried, then they'd made love and fallen asleep in each other's arms. What would she give if every day with Lee could be as wonderful as that one had been? If only he could be happy spending days like that with her instead of always being so obsessed with gaining status, fame, and fortune, they would still be together.

As she parked in front of the Humanities building at the junior college, she wiped away bitter tears and hurried inside so she could take a few minutes before the lecture to clear her mind of all the what-ifs about her marriage. She took a seat in the back of the room and closed her eyes, mentally repeating the self-affirming mantra she'd composed to help focus her energies on the positive things in her life. When she opened her eyes, a man who seemed vaguely familiar was staring at her from behind the podium in the front of the room.

Their gazes met briefly before Professor Avery, the

history professor who'd given the first lecture, walked up and began talking to him. The man glanced in her direction once more while he conversed with the professor, which made her think he recognized her too. Where had she seen him before?

He wasn't unattractive by any means, but she didn't really think anyone would describe him as handsome either. The most notable thing about him was his height, which Jess estimated at well over six feet. His hair was the same medium brown shade as the jacket and slacks that didn't quite seem to fit his large frame. Nothing memorable at all about him really, but there was still something that made Jess think they'd met before.

When all the lecture attendees had arrived, Professor Avery closed the door and returned to the podium. "Good evening, and welcome to the second installment of our Revolutionary War series. Our guest speaker tonight is Mr. Noah Hamilton, chairman of the history department at Espanola High School."

Darn it, his name didn't help jog her memory at all. She might've heard it before but had no idea where or when. As he stepped up to the podium, his gaze met hers again momentarily, and she got the feeling he was looking for a reaction from her, as if he knew who she was and wanted to see if she recognized him as well. Who the devil was he?

As soon as he began speaking, she knew.

Although it was possible they'd had more than one class together in high school, she remembered talking to him only once when he'd complimented her on an impassioned essay she'd written about tobacco company lawsuits that she'd read aloud in her sophomore English class. She recalled thinking back then that his voice reminded her of the wind in the trees outside her bedroom window, a soothing whisper that had lulled her to sleep for as long as she could remember. After she'd thanked him for the compliment on the essay, he'd hesitated a moment, and she'd had a sudden fear that he was going to ask her out.

She couldn't remember which Lee-clone she'd been dating at the time, but it didn't really matter. She wouldn't have gone out with Noah Hamilton even if she'd been unattached, because he hadn't measured up to the macho standards she'd always had for her boyfriends. She wasn't sure if Noah had sensed her reluctance or had just changed his mind, but he had simply told her goodbye and left. She couldn't remember ever talking to him again.

His lecture topic for the night was the debate that had gone on between the Federalists and the Republicans as to what direction the fledgling American country had needed to take after the war, and Jess became engrossed as she listened to the uncommon facts and little-known details Noah relayed to them in his velvety voice. An hour had passed before she knew it, and his closing remarks were followed by enthusiastic applause from everyone in the room.

She could see she'd have to wait in line for a chance to speak to him, so she slipped into the restroom across the hall to powder her nose and put on some lipstick, feeling silly as she did it. All she wanted to do was tell him how much she'd enjoyed his talk and let him know she remembered him. So why was she primping like a schoolgirl with her pulse racing all of a sudden?

She dried her palms on the seat of her jeans as she waited behind a blue-haired lady who was busy telling Noah how much he reminded her of her late husband Maurice. Had it not been for the lady's impatient grandson finally pulling her away, she might never have released Noah's hand. As soon as his admirer reluctantly moved aside and he saw Jess, Noah's blue eyes smiled at her even before his mouth had time to join them.

"Jessica Hunter. I thought it was you."

She held out her hand and returned his smile. "It's good to see you again, Noah. I loved your lecture tonight."

He clasped her hand in both of his, and she felt an odd sensation at the base of her spine that intensified when she noticed the bare ring finger on his left hand.

"Thank you, I'm glad you enjoyed it. The Revolutionary War is a subject I could talk about endlessly, which is what my students often accuse me of doing."

She laughed. "Well, they clearly don't know how lucky they are to have such a captivating speaker for an instructor. You were definitely a hit with this group tonight. I think that last lady intends to run for president of your fan club."

He looked embarrassed. "Thanks, Jess. That's nice of you to say."

Their gazes met again, and Jess was transported back in time to that moment in high school when she'd thought he was going to ask her out. Maybe it was because she felt guilty for the reluctance she'd felt at the prospect back then and wished she'd been nicer to him, but she decided there would be a different outcome this time.

"Noah, would you like to go somewhere and get a cup of coffee? I'd love the chance to talk to you some more."

His expression was a mixture of relief, surprise and delight. "Oh…yes. Thanks." He cleared his throat and turned to stuff some papers into a leather binder. "I'll hurry so I won't hold you up."

"Take your time. No rush."

He glanced up at her, and she had to resist the urge to squeeze his hand and reassure him that she wouldn't change her mind about going. When they got out to the parking lot, they discovered they'd parked right next to each other. Jess told him to follow her to a coffee shop nearby that stayed open late for the college crowd.

As she drove the few blocks to the café, Jess questioned her actions but didn't regret them a bit. Noah's obvious excitement over having coffee with her was more than a little flattering, and she could tell she would enjoy talking to him once he relaxed a little. He seemed so sweet and unassuming, totally unlike all her past dates—not to mention her estranged husband. Why had she always picked macho, extroverted guys who'd all ended up disappointing her?

She parked outside the Java Joint, thinking of the old adage about those who didn't learn from history being doomed to repeat it. Smiling as she got out and went in, she decided it was quite the appropriate mindset for having coffee with a silken-voiced history buff.

Chapter Seven

The Java Joint was laid out in the deliberately cozy style such places seemed to favor, with several couches and overstuffed chairs arranged to maximize conversation. Jess and Noah opted for a small table in a quiet corner and gave the waitress their order for two coffees.

"I guess I should've ordered decaf this late at night," Noah said, "but I just don't like it. It's probably all in my head, but it never seems to taste as good as regular coffee."

Jess nodded. "I know. There seems to be something missing. Besides the caffeine, of course." They both laughed, and she could see him relax a little. "Catch me up on what you've been doing since high school, Noah."

"Okay, but there's not much to tell." He looked at his hands on the table in front of him. "I got my education degree at Florida State and taught at a middle school in St. Pete until two years ago when I came here to visit my brother and his wife. I liked the community and heard they had a good school system, so I applied for a job at Espanola High School, and here I am."

"You must be an excellent teacher if they made you head of the history department after only two years."

"It's a small school." He gave a little shrug. "But

not many people love history the way I do. I guess the administrators figured anyone so obsessed would have to be dedicated."

Their coffee arrived in enormous mugs that Jess knew she'd have to use both hands to lift. She looked from the monster cups to the dubious expression on Noah's face, and they both laughed again.

"Maybe this is their way of helping coffee drinkers bulk up," she said.

"I may need to stretch before taking a drink so I won't pull something." He reached for the pitcher of cream and flushed when his hand bumped hers. "Oh, sorry. You go ahead."

She'd never known a man who blushed so easily. Maybe it was because of her present appreciation for qualities that differed so much from Lee's arrogance, but she found Noah's shy awkwardness surprisingly sexy.

"I really enjoyed your lecture, Noah. You definitely have a gift for speaking. Do you plan to teach at the college level in the future?"

"No, I honestly enjoy teaching high school." He fiddled with the container of sugar packets between them but didn't use any. "My advanced students are great, and occasionally I get a prodigy who decides they want to teach because of my class. That's always gratifying and makes me feel as if I'm making a small contribution to the world's future."

"I think that's wonderful, and it's no small contribution you're making. Teachers are a vital resource we'd all be in trouble without."

The color in his cheeks deepened again. "Thanks, Jess. Tell me about you now."

"I'm a copyeditor at the *Espanola Times*. I'd like to write myself someday, but I enjoy what I'm doing now."

He lifted his cup to take a sip. "How did you come to move here from Tampa?"

"My husband's family lives here."

She realized her gaffe when he inhaled his coffee and started to cough.

"Oh, Noah, I'm sorry." She reached across the table to pat him on the back. "I should have said my *ex*-husband. We're in the process of getting a divorce."

When he could breathe normally again, he said, "It's okay. I just had a mental image of my head being used for batting practice by your outraged husband. Or did you end up with a football player?"

"What makes you think that?" she asked, although she knew the answer.

"As I recall, all your boyfriends seemed to hang around the gym a lot. It got kind of hard to tell them apart after a while." He smiled and wiped his eyes with a napkin since they were still watering from his coffee aspiration.

Jess had to laugh at her predictability. "Actually, I had one boyfriend who didn't play any kind of sports. Steve Donovan—remember him? He rode a motorcycle."

"Oh, yes. But didn't he get kicked off the football team for a…jockstrap violation or something similar?"

She laughed harder. "I don't remember, but it's possible. I think he liked the gas fumes from his Harley a little too much."

Noah studied the interior of his coffee cup. "So which one of them did you end up marrying?"

Lee's image appeared instantly in her mind, but she shoved it aside. "Nobody from high school. I met him at Georgia Tech. He's a reporter for the *Espanola Times*."

Noah's eyebrows went up. "A writer? That's a little off the beaten path for you, isn't it?"

"Well, he's a sportswriter. And he played football until he injured his knee during our freshman year."

"Oh, that makes sense then. Sorry it didn't work out." He didn't look a bit sorry, and she felt that odd sensation in her spine again. "I never understood what a smart girl like you saw in those guys anyway."

"I didn't understand it either, but at least I finally wised up. Better late than never, right?"

"Right." He gave her that indecisive look again. "Jess, there's something I want you...I mean, there's something I want to tell you."

"What is it?"

He stared at his hands a few seconds before looking up at her with a sigh. "I wanted to ask you out the whole time we were in high school, but I didn't have the guts. I've always regretted it."

"I wish we'd known each other better, Noah. I mean that." She didn't want to lie and tell him she would have gone out with him if he'd asked, but she also didn't want to hurt his feelings.

"I may be stupid sometimes, but I always try to learn from my mistakes." He took a deep breath. "Would you like to have dinner with me tomorrow night?"

She'd been with Lee for so long that the idea of going on a real date with another man brought on a wave of guilt that caused a knot in her stomach and made her heart beat erratically in her chest. She didn't know if she could do it at first. But then she looked at the sweet man sitting across from her who was literally holding his breath as he waited for her answer, and her decision became easy.

"I'd love to, Noah."

His face displayed his elation, and she was again flattered that spending time with her clearly meant so much to him. What would it hurt to have dinner with him anyway? He was an old friend whose company she enjoyed, and all they were going to do was share a meal and some intelligent conversation. There was nothing wrong with that, so she had no reason to feel guilty.

Right. So why was the knot in her stomach getting bigger by the second?

****

When she got home and saw the message light blinking on her answering machine, something told her it was from Lee, and the knot in her stomach doubled in size. She sat on the side of the bed with a sigh and punched the replay button.

"Hey, baby. I called to see if you can take me to the airport in the morning so I won't have to leave my car there over the weekend while I'm gone. Call me when you get home and let me know."

The machine beeped, and Jess looked at Ming in disbelief. "He's completely lost his mind, hasn't he?" She got only a yawn in reply from her cat, so she picked up the phone and called her demented spouse.

"Hey, baby," he said. "Where you been?"

"You're unbelievable. Not only are you crazy for thinking I'll take you to the airport, it's none of your business where I've been."

"Why can't you take me? You can just drop me off at the front and won't even have to park."

"Lee, I'm not taking you to the damn airport so you can fly off to an interview for the job I threw you out over."

He sighed. "I can't believe you don't want me to get this job. It's *Sports Spotlight*, baby. They're the axis of the sportswriting world."

"You mean the *apex*, Lee. And I wouldn't care if this interview was with Donald Trump because he wanted you to write his personal sports page for him every morning. But since I know you don't have a clue about what I mean, just forget it."

"Fine, I'll take a cab. So where'd you go tonight?"

She looked at the ceiling as if for divine inspiration and decided to tell him the truth. Maybe she'd stop feeling guilty about it then.

"Not that it's any of your business, but I went to a lecture at the junior college. The speaker turned out to be an old friend from high school, and we went out for coffee afterward. We're having dinner together tomorrow night too."

"A lecture, huh? Sure you can handle that much excitement on a weeknight?"

Angry heat washed over her. "Thank you *so* much, Lee. I was hoping you'd say something like that."

He laughed. "Anytime, baby. You know I'm always here for you."

She hung up feeling almost more incredulous than angry. Was she supposed to believe he wanted her to take him back if he was so overjoyed with his new job prospect that he couldn't even be bothered to care if she had a date? If this magazine made him an offer, he'd probably be more than happy to sign the divorce papers as soon as he got back from New York.

"Well, fine," she said as she picked up Ming and sat cross-legged in the middle of the bed. "Now there's definitely no reason for me to feel guilty about going out with Noah. Lee knows about it and couldn't care less."

Ming ran away when the first tears fell on her head.

****

Jess woke the next morning with swollen eyes and a headache that was compounded by self-recrimination because she'd pulled her hair while crying herself to sleep—the first setback she'd had since she'd started her Habit Reversal Training. She was disappointed in herself for slipping, but she also felt stupid and hypocritical for crying over a man she'd thrown out twice and was supposedly trying to divorce.

She had never been one of those women who seemed to thrive on conflict and thought it was flattering for their men to behave like jealous idiots. Even in high school, she'd never played the silly games other girls played to make their boyfriends jealous. So why did it suddenly matter so much to her that Lee didn't care if she was with another man? She should be glad and hope it meant he was ready to stop fighting the divorce. But that wasn't the way it made her feel at all, and she didn't know what to make of that.

She was late for work because she had to lie down with cucumber-extract pads on her eyes, hoping it would keep anyone from noticing her puffy eyes. At least she didn't have to worry about running into Lee all day. She'd also decided not to tell Deb anything about Noah yet since she tended to overreact about anything to do with men. If she found out that Noah was cooking dinner for Jess at his apartment that night, Deb would definitely read more into it than she should.

If it had been any man other than Noah, Jess would never have agreed to a first date alone with him at his apartment. But she hadn't thought twice about accepting when he'd offered to cook dinner for them and promised her the best lasagna she'd ever tasted. Maybe she was being naïve, but something about the way he looked at her made her believe she could trust him. Besides, if Noah did turn out to be a serial killer, at least Lee should be racked with guilt for not trying to stop her from going out with him.

She got home in plenty of time to get ready and primp her little heart out. Despite her conflicting feelings about Lee, she couldn't deny that she was truly looking forward to seeing Noah again. Just as she was putting a spritz of cologne between her breasts, Ming padded regally into the bathroom and eyed her mistress in the mirror with what Jess could have sworn was disapproval. She put down the atomizer and turned to frown at the cat.

"I'm only putting it there because it's a pulse point, so stop looking at me like that. And since when are you in league with Mr. Big Apple anyway?"

Ming's response was an almost imperceptible twitch of one ear and a downright impertinent flick of her tail.

"Oh, go wash your face for the hundredth time today and let me get dressed in peace."

She took a green silk blouse from her closet and had trouble buttoning it because her hands were shaking. What was wrong with her? She hadn't been so nervous about a date since the first time Lee had asked her out when they were in college.

"Oh, you go away too," she said to Lee's image in her head. "You're not invited on this date."

Resigned to the inevitability of his specter hovering somewhere nearby all night, Jess sat in front of her makeup mirror and eyed her hair with disdain. Despite the twenty minutes she'd already spent trying to get both sides to curl in exactly the same way, the hair at her left temple insisted on flipping out instead of back. Good thing she'd hidden the scissors from herself or she would have already lopped off the offensive swatch. With a sigh, she flipped the mirror over to the magnified side so her hair wasn't visible.

"Out of sight, out of mind," she said, then sighed again. "If only that were true when it came to Lee."

She left in plenty of time to make the fifteen-minute drive to Stoneridge, a much more upscale apartment complex than she would have expected a teacher to live in. She found Noah's apartment easily and rang the doorbell, feeling both excited and anxious about seeing him again.

"Hi, Jess," he said when he answered the door. "Come on in." He gave her another of those intense looks, as if he couldn't quite believe she was really there.

"Your apartment is beautiful," she said, looking around. "No one would ever guess it belonged to a bachelor."

"Thank you. My sister-in-law is an interior decorator and did it for me gratis." He showed her to a seat at the marble-topped bar separating the living room from the kitchen. "Dinner's almost ready. Would you like an aperitif?"

"I'd love one," she said, still admiring the décor. The rooms were filled with warm colors complemented by the soft lighting, and the furniture was a creamy beige leather that looked hungry for a body to surround. Jess even recognized some framed art she thought might not be reproductions.

Noah handed her a glass of sherry. "I thought we'd eat outside and enjoy this cool spell while it lasts."

She turned to look through the sliding glass doors at the table set for two out on the balcony. "How lovely, Noah. Thank you so much for doing all this."

He picked up his own glass and walked around the bar to stand beside her chair. "I was glad to do it. Until I saw you standing in the doorway, I kept thinking maybe I'd dreamed it all and you weren't really coming."

"Well, that lasagna certainly smells like a dream. Where did you learn to cook?"

He took a sip of wine and shrugged. "Self-taught out of desperation. My parents were away on business a lot, and we had a housekeeper who was a lousy cook. When my brother threatened to commit suicide if we had to eat her tuna casserole one more time, I took up cooking to save his life."

Jess laughed. "What kind of business are your parents in?"

"They're partners in a consulting firm. Experts at telling people the most efficient way to manage their companies, yet too busy to manage their own family." When her eyebrows went up slightly at his tone, he looked embarrassed. "Sorry about that. I'm still working on teaching myself not to resent growing up with absentee parents."

She touched his arm. "No need to apologize. I think a lot of problems could be avoided if more people realized how deeply children are affected by what their parents do or don't do."

He looked from her hand on his arm to her eyes. "I always knew you were a compassionate person. That's why I never understood why you dated all those Neanderthals."

"Well, God forbid we should be held accountable for what we did as teenagers, right?"

"I don't know about that. I was pretty much the same as a teenager. Maybe that's why I never seemed to fit in."

"Yet you ended up teaching high school and seem to enjoy it."

He nodded. "I do, but I must admit I have a soft spot for the kids like me. The ones everyone thinks are weird."

"I didn't think you were weird, Noah. Just shy."

He looked as though he were going to say something about that, then he nodded toward the balcony. "Let's sit outside while we wait for the lasagna to finish cooking. There's usually a breeze this time of day."

She followed him outside and was delighted to find there was indeed a wonderfully cool breeze that carried the scent of Confederate jasmine to them from somewhere nearby. Noah had placed Japanese lanterns along the balcony's railing, and Tony Bennett was singing the old standards softly in the background.

"This is all so nice," she said as he pulled out her chair for her. "I envy you for having it to enjoy all the time."

"You're welcome to come share it with me anytime. I mean that."

"I might just take you up on it. Do you get breezes like this even when it's so hot in the summer?"

He nodded. "There's a lake on the other side of those pine trees over there. I think it's the reason for the cooler air."

A timer went off in the kitchen and he excused himself to get the lasagna. Jess finished her sherry and took the glass inside so she could offer to help, but he insisted she do nothing but sit on the balcony and enjoy the evening. He'd also made a salad and had a wonderful crusty bread to go with the lasagna, which proved to be every bit as good as he'd promised. While they ate, they talked about their favorite books, movies and music, and Jess wasn't surprised to find they had a lot in common.

"Do you think you'll stay here in Espanola after your divorce is final?" Noah asked.

"Oh, I suppose so," she said. "I've never been exceptionally close to my family, so I don't really miss Tampa much. And I enjoy my job at the newspaper."

"You don't think it might be awkward to keep working with your husband after you're divorced?"

"To be honest," Jess said, "I don't expect him to be working there too much longer. He's always had his line baited for much bigger fish. The kind that swim in New York."

"Oh, I see." He seemed pleased to hear of Lee's big city aspirations. "Well, I'm glad you plan to stay here, and I can't say I blame you about not missing Tampa. I fell in love with our quaint little town the first time I saw it. It reminds me a lot of the villages in New England."

"I'll have to take your word for it since I've never been out of the Southeast. Have you done a lot of traveling?"

"Quite a bit actually. I've been to all fifty states, three provinces in Canada, and to Mexico and Europe."

Jess's brows went up. "Wow, I'm impressed. And green with envy."

"My parents liked to take my brother and me on extravagant vacations to make up for all the time they were gone otherwise." He looked a bit sheepish. "Oops, there I go again."

Jess smiled. "No problem. I understand completely about lingering bitterness. But that's definitely not a subject for a first date, so let's talk about something else, okay?"

"Actually, I need to excuse myself for a moment to get something else from the kitchen." He stood and picked up their plates. "I won't be long."

He came back with an amazing chocolate mousse he'd made for dessert. When Jess tasted it, she told him she must have been killed in a wreck on the way over, because she was most assuredly in heaven. By the time they finished dessert, the breeze had become chilly enough to move them back inside. Noah brought the wine and poured them both another glass when he sat beside Jess on the sofa.

"I probably shouldn't drink anymore," she said. "Especially since I have to drive."

"I hope you're not ready to leave yet. It's still so early."

She took the glass from him. "I guess a couple of

sips to warm me up would be all right. I can't believe how cool it got out there this late in May."

He smiled and turned toward her on the couch. "So tell me, when are you going to let me read something you've written?"

She laughed and rolled her eyes. "Probably never. I'm too chicken to let anyone read it."

"Not even your husband?"

Jess's smile vanished. "No, and nothing I wrote would interest him anyway. We have vastly different tastes about most things."

"But don't you read what he writes?"

She took a sip of wine and stared into her glass. "Yes, but that's different. I edit his articles for him."

"Does he even know you write?"

She looked up at him in surprise and wondered how he'd guessed. "No, but I'm sure he'd say my time would be better spent editing copy for sportswriting's golden boy, Lee Cassady." As soon as she said his name, Lee's specter appeared in her head and glared at her.

"Then he must be just as stupid as the guys you dated in high school," Noah said. "I'm glad you finally realized it."

She sighed. "I'm sorry, Noah, but I don't feel comfortable talking about him. Can we please change the subject?"

"Of course we can." He drained his glass and took hers to set them both aside, then he took a deep breath before looking at her again. "Let's talk about how stupid *I* was not to ever tell you I'd been crazy about you since we were in junior high."

Her heart suddenly felt confined in her chest.

"Noah—"

"Please, Jess. Let me finish before the wine wears off and I lose my nerve." He took both her hands in his. "I remember the exact day I knew you were the girl for me. We were in Mr. Tolbert's seventh grade science class, and someone had brought in their pet snake and a live mouse to feed it. Several of the other girls claimed they felt sorry for the poor mouse, but all they did was giggle and wait for the snake to eat it. But you, Jess…I remember how your eyes seemed to have green fire in them when you pushed all the kids aside and reached into the case to rescue the mouse. And the look on your face dared any of them to stop you when you took it to the window and let it go. I'd never seen anyone so brave or so beautiful."

Jess remembered that day, and it broke her heart that she had no recollection of Noah even being there. How could she have gone to school with him for so long without realizing how he felt? Had she really been that self-absorbed? Was that what she had in common with the kind of guys she'd always dated?

"Noah, I'm so sorry. I didn't know."

"It wasn't your fault. I was the one who didn't have the guts to even speak to you, but that's why I'm telling you all this now. I've thought about you so many times over the years, and I swore to myself that I'd tell you how I felt if I ever saw you again. I just hope I haven't scared you away now."

"You haven't scared me," she said. "Who wouldn't be happy to know someone cared for them so much?"

"Even if that someone still doesn't quite fit in anywhere?"

"You fit in just fine with me, Noah."

"Jess…" He paused and glanced at their hands before looking into her eyes. "Would you mind if I kissed you?"

She could see how afraid he was that she would reject him after he'd just opened his heart to her. For much the same reason she'd risked the scorn of her peers to rescue that terrified mouse all those years ago, she pulled one of her hands from his and put it on his cheek.

"I'd mind if you didn't."

He leaned toward her hesitantly, but once their lips met, his arms went around her and pulled her against him. Jess had always been a big fan of kissing, and Noah was surprisingly good at it. There was also something magical about kissing someone for the first time, discovering the feel and the taste of their mouth and the excitement of knowing they were discovering yours as well. Jess felt herself responding as the kiss deepened, but when one of his hands drifted down her waistline to her thigh, she was struck by a wave of guilt so strong that she pushed on his chest and stopped him.

"I can't do this, Noah." She moved away from him on the couch, her heart trying to beat its way out of her chest. "I shouldn't have kissed you. I'm still Lee's wife until the divorce is final, and I'd never be able to live with myself if I were unfaithful."

"Do you still have feelings for him?" He didn't look at her. "Is that why you feel guilty for being with me?"

Her denial stuck in her throat, because she couldn't lie about it. "I'll always have feelings for him, but I wouldn't have filed for divorce if I honestly thought there was hope for us."

He appeared relieved at her answer. "Then I can wait until you're divorced. I've already waited fourteen years, so what's a little longer?" He took her hand again. "I'll try not to do anything to make you uncomfortable if you'll promise to let me see you again."

"It's a deal," she said. "No matter what happens, I wouldn't want to lose your friendship."

They talked about their jobs and other less personal subjects, and she could tell he was relieved that everything was out in the open between them. He was attentive and funny and completely unpretentious, and Jess enjoyed talking to him so much that she had to make herself leave when it was time to go.

"I still think I should follow you home to make sure you're all right," he said when he walked her out to her car.

"That's sweet of you, Noah, but it's not necessary. I'll be fine." She put her purse inside on the seat and turned to smile at him. "Thank you for a wonderful evening."

He looked at her as if he were trying to engrave her image with his eyes. "No, thank *you*, Jess. For one of the best nights of my life."

She stretched up to kiss him on the cheek. "There'll be more. I promised, remember?"

"Don't worry," he said. "I'd never forget something as important as that."

She drove home with her mind reeling and her emotions in an uproar. There was so much to process that she didn't know what to think about first—that Noah had cared so much about her for all those years and she'd had no idea, that he clearly wanted a romantic relationship with her now, or that she wasn't sure she could keep everything at a manageable level until she was divorced.

Noah was a wonderful man that she loved talking to, and she also couldn't deny how enthralling it was to be with a man who was focused completely on her. The way he listened to her and the way he looked at her made her feel like the most beautiful, interesting woman in the world. She liked that feeling. She liked it a lot. And she found herself wondering why she had caused herself to miss out on it for so long by always choosing men who were too wrapped up in themselves to care about her.

Noah was nothing like her previous boyfriends, and that might be exactly what she needed. Maybe it was time she gave sweet, sensitive men a try. And since Lee was too busy making a name for himself in New York to even care if she dated other men, it definitely didn't make sense for her to feel any kind of ridiculous loyalty to him. There had definitely been a spark present when Noah kissed her. Maybe if they took things slow, that spark could grow into a real flame and ward off any residual guilt that tried to keep her from finding happiness with a man who actually deserved her devotion.

By the time she got home, she felt as if she'd resolved things pretty well in her mind and was feeling much better about it all. So it wasn't until she was getting into bed and noticed the blinking message light on the answering machine that Lee's recorded voice from a thousand miles away tossed all her rationalizations and ambitious decisions straight out the window.

"Hey, baby. I made it here in one piece, so don't spend the insurance money just yet. And don't forget that I love you even while you're pretending to hate me. See you when I get back."

Chapter Eight

Jess had a bagel and a generous helping of confusion with her coffee the next morning. She'd stayed up late trying to make sense of either Lee's baffling behavior or her conflicting emotions about Noah, and she'd succeeded in neither. Sometime around three that morning, she'd fallen asleep and dreamt she was at her junior prom, dancing with Noah in her wedding dress, then Lee had shown up in full football gear and tried to cut in. The dream ended with the three of them—all naked of course—eating éclairs at her kitchen table.

After a fruitless morning of trying to complete at least one task, she bit the bullet and called Deb to tell her about the date with Noah.

"Oh my God, Jess," Deb said. "What do you think you're doing keeping things like this to yourself? No wonder you pull out your hair. When are you seeing him again?"

"Tonight, I hope. One of his students is in the production of *The Taming of the Shrew* they're doing at the Espanola Playhouse. He's trying to get me a ticket to go with him."

"Ooh, a Shakespeare man. Much better for you than the Cro-Magnon man you married."

Jess laughed. "You really should ask Thad about writing that humor column. You're way funnier than

Bubba Beerbelly's Redneck Report."

"Don't try to change the subject. This Noah guy could be just what you need to get over the jerkwad. He sounds perfect for you, and you said he gets your blood going too, right?"

"No, I said I was attracted to him even though he's not my usual type."

"Same thing," Deb said. "And since your track record with the beefcake boys is so crappy, I think you definitely need to give the intellectual type a try."

Jess rubbed Ming's back with her bare foot. "It's not that simple, Deb. I'm not even divorced yet, and I have no idea how much longer Lee plans to drag it out."

"You think he'll be moving to New York if he gets the job with *Sports Spotlight*?"

"I don't know. Maybe."

"Well, if he moves without you, I'm pretty sure that's considered abandonment or something. Then you'll have grounds for divorce and can be rid of him."

"Yeah, I know." Jess sighed. "He'll probably be happy to sign the papers if he gets this job, which I'm sure he will."

"Well, there you go. Then your patient paramour can unleash all that latent passion on you. They say the quiet ones are real tigers in bed, you know."

Jess promised to call her in the morning and hung up in much better spirits if no less confused. Noah called a little later to say he'd gotten her a ticket for the play and would be there to pick her up at six. She still had plenty of time before she needed to start getting dressed, so she decided to work on the short story she'd been revising for the umpteenth time.

She opened the file on her computer and spent the

next couple of hours blissfully lost in the world she'd created for her characters. She loved the way it felt to be completely in control of everything that happened to them and to dictate every word that was spoken. If only she could control the events in her own life the same way.

When she noticed the time, she couldn't believe how quickly it had passed. With a wistful sigh, she resolved once again to do an Internet search for writing contests and force herself to actually submit something this time. She'd come close to entering a short story contest a few months earlier, until her mother had called with the news that Elise's wedding photographer felt sure that *Bride* magazine would want to use Elise's pictures in a feature on Southern weddings. In the face of her sister's latest triumph, Jess had lost her nerve.

"Who am I kidding?" she said to Ming, who'd been sleeping in her lap while she wrote. "Even if I find the guts to enter anything and actually manage to win something in a contest, I can just hear Mother's patronizing assessment of such a minor success compared to Elise's accomplishments. And can you imagine what she would say if I were to enter and lose?"

Ming stretched languidly and curled up again.

"Yeah, I know," Jess said. "I don't want to think about it either."

The ironic thing was, her mother's criticism had actually been the catalyst for the idea behind the story that was her best effort. One stormy night the previous summer, after Marjorie had called and lambasted her for refusing to participate in the Junior League's annual fashion show—the least she could do since her own mother was the chairperson—Marjorie had asked her for the millionth time why she couldn't be more civic-minded and socially conscious like her sister.

Jess had hung up and written the first draft of "Midsummer Shower," an eerie tale of an unfortunate girl whose mother drives her insane with her constant disapproval and neglect. Through a one-sided conversation between the girl and someone in an abandoned cabin during a storm, it's revealed that the girl was also victimized by a predatory boyfriend whose corpse turns out to be her companion in the cabin.

Although Jess had begun writing it for cathartic reasons, once she'd gotten into the story, the girl had come alive for her so much that the character ended up nothing like herself at all, and the victimization and death tangents had practically written themselves. For all the story's disturbing pathos, Jess really liked the way it had turned out.

As she shut down her computer to get ready for her date, she wondered if she should write a story about a heroine with a troubled marriage. Maybe it would help her figure out what to do about Lee, because she definitely wasn't having any luck on her own. Every time she thought she was sure she wanted him out of her life, he'd do or say something to make her think he really cared about her after all.

****

Noah arrived ten minutes early, so Jess ushered him into the living room to wait while she finished getting ready. When Ming jumped onto his lap and made herself at home, Jess was flabbergasted at her cat's show of affection.

"She's never taken to anyone like this before," Jess

said. "And especially not a man. You should be flattered, Noah."

"Oh, I am, believe me." He smoothed Ming's fur and got a contented purr in return. "I know how temperamental Siamese cats can be. We had a pair that Disney could have used as models for the ones in *Lady and the Tramp*."

"Oh, I love that movie," Jess said. "It's my second-favorite Disney flick after *The Little Mermaid*." She walked over and opened a door on the entertainment center. "I have the entire Disney collection. I know every word of every song, but don't ask me to sing unless you want Ming to run away and hide."

Noah laughed. "Okay, but maybe we can watch a couple of them sometime and you can sing for me then. I haven't seen any of those movies since I was a kid, and I really wouldn't mind watching them again."

"It's a deal." She closed the cabinet. "I know they're kids' movies, but I'll always love them. Lee makes fun of—" She bit her lip and looked at him sheepishly. "I'd better finish getting ready so we won't be late."

She looked around the room as she left to see where Lee's specter was hovering, and she vowed to thrash herself if she mentioned his name again for the rest of the night. When she came back to the living room a few minutes later, Noah was standing in front of the mantel and she realized she should've put away her wedding picture. He turned slowly from the image of her wedded bliss and looked at her as if he couldn't believe she wanted to go anywhere with him when she had a husband who looked like Lee.

"Let's go, Noah." She took his hand. "I'm ready

for an evening out with my favorite history buff."

He smiled and tucked her hand in the crook of his arm. "In that case, would you like to hear how I got interested in history to begin with?"

"Oh, definitely," she said as they left. "I love listening to you talk. You have the sexiest voice I've ever heard."

"Thanks." He blushed only a little. "Anyway, my mother thought we were distant relatives of Alexander Hamilton's until she commissioned a genealogy study that proved we weren't. But I'd already read a great deal about him as a result and found out what a brilliant, amazing man he was. I've been a devoted Hamiltonian ever since."

He told her all about his favorite patriot as they drove to the play, and she couldn't help noticing how much more confident he seemed when he was talking about history, as if he were in his element. They arrived at the theatre with time to spare before the play began, so he introduced her to several of his students and a few other teachers who were also in attendance. Jess thought they all looked rather surprised to meet her and seemed to watch them closely as she and Noah took their seats, so she asked him about it.

"Actually," he said, "I thought they handled the shock pretty well. No one passed out or anything."

"What are you talking about?" She frowned over his shoulder at the middle-aged English teacher she'd just met who was whispering to her husband while staring openly at them from a few rows away.

Noah laughed a little self-consciously. "Well, I'm pretty sure they all think I'm gay. I guess I really can't blame them. I've never been married or shown any interest in the single women on the faculty. They're probably trying to figure out whether you're a relative or a pity date. There could even be some money riding on it."

"Oh, good grief. Don't they have anything better to do than stick their noses in other people's business?" She realized how naïve that sounded from the dubious look he gave her, so she said, "Well, I don't like gossips. What do you say we put an end to their speculation?"

She put her hand on his cheek and pulled his face to hers so she could give him a kiss that lasted long enough to remove all question as to why she was with him.

"Well, that ought to do it," he said with a broad smile. "We'll be the talk of the teachers' lounge Monday morning."

Jess looked up dreamily. "That's always been my life's goal."

They both laughed, and she held his hand as the house lights went down for the play to begin. He squeezed her fingers and she reminded herself that he deserved her attention much more than He-Whose-Name-Could-Not-Be-Mentioned.

Noah's student, a handsome boy named Derek, portrayed Petruchio in the play, and Jess enjoyed the comical rendition set in a 1950s-era Padua, complete with jukeboxes and poodle skirts. When they went to get a drink at intermission, a pair of female students Noah had introduced Jess to earlier got behind them in line, and one of them tugged on Noah's jacket sleeve.

"Mr. Hamilton, Ashley doesn't believe me about Madison being a Federalist. He was, wasn't he?" She blinked at him with glittery pink lids.

"Actually, Lauren," Noah replied, "Madison wrote *The Federalist Papers*, but he changed his affiliation later on, debatably because of his friendship with Thomas Jefferson. We can talk about it in class on Monday if you girls will remind me."

"We will," they said in unison.

Jess had to bite her lip to keep from laughing, because it was so obvious that Noah was completely unaware of the girls' adoration. He ordered coffees for them when they reached the counter and nodded politely to the wide-eyed girls as they walked away. Jess made it all the way back to their seats before giving in to her laughter.

"What?" Noah peered around them. "Did I miss something?"

"Oh, you missed plenty, Mr. Hamilton." Jess tried not to spill her coffee. "Your coworkers might wonder about your sexual orientation, but your students obviously don't."

"What do you mean?"

"Noah, those girls have a major crush on you. You can't see it?"

He scoffed. "Nonsense. They were just trying to earn a few brownie points."

"Uh-huh, and you think a girl who carries a purse that says 'Born to Shop' goes around discussing American history with her girlfriends?"

"Well, maybe I just did an exceptionally good job of sparking their interest in our country's foundation." He continued to look serious until Jess had to cover her mouth to keep from spitting coffee on him, then he laughed with her. "Okay, I know that's not likely. But

I'm sure it just has to do with some sort of older man mystique and has nothing to do with me. I'm not exactly heartthrob material."

"Don't say that, Noah. You have beautiful eyes and a heavenly voice that makes my heart throb quite a bit."

A smile spread slowly across his face. "I'm extremely glad to hear that."

He held her hand throughout the rest of the play, and several times she caught him looking at her instead of the actors on the stage. When the play was over, they waited in the lobby for the actors to come out so Noah could congratulate Derek, and Jess could tell the boy was thrilled that Noah had come to see him.

"Apparently, Mr. Hamilton," Jess said as they got in the car, "you're a big hit with your male students as well. You must be a wonderful teacher."

"I do love teaching, and I think they appreciate having someone who actually wants to be there with them. Too many teachers act more like they're serving a life sentence."

When they pulled into her driveway, Jess didn't hesitate to invite him inside, but he looked unsure. "I don't want to make you uncomfortable the way I did last night," he said. "I think I should just walk you to the door and say goodnight there."

She shook her head. "I'm not worried about being alone with you. Besides, I'm sure Ming wants to see you again."

"Are you sure, Jess? I..." He looked down a moment. "I can't promise I won't try to kiss you."

"I'll risk it, Noah."

He smiled, then he got out and came around to open her door for her. She took his hand as she got out and kept holding it as they walked to the front porch. Just as they reached the steps, she heard a car in the driveway and turned around in time to see Lee jump out of his Mustang and charge across the lawn toward them.

"What the *hell* is going on, Jess!"

"Lee, stop yelling like a maniac." She moved quickly to intercept him before he reached Noah. "What are you doing here?"

He stopped and glared at her. "This is *my* house, and I came to see *my* wife! Who the hell is this guy?"

"I told you when you called the other day that I was having dinner with an old friend. We went to a play together tonight."

He looked incredulous. "I thought you meant an old *girl*friend! Damn it, Jess, you think I wouldn't have said anything about you going out with another man?"

She did her best to ignore the infuriating joy that invaded her heart at knowing that he did care about what she did after all because this wasn't the time to examine her feelings about it, but she would definitely have to think about them later.

"Well, it shouldn't make a difference to you either way, Lee, because we're getting a divorce. What I do is none of your business anymore." She turned to walk back to Noah, who looked as though he wished the Earth would open up and swallow him.

Lee grabbed her arm and stopped her. "Like hell it's not my business! You're still my wife, and I'm not letting any man put his hands on you!"

She whirled around to face him again. "Well, maybe I'll come up with some story about being drugged and not knowing what I'm doing, then it won't matter. Right, Lee?"

He moved her aside and started toward Noah. "Why don't we see if your boyfriend's willing to get his ass kicked for you!"

Noah held up his hands and took a step back. "Look, I don't want any trouble with you, but I intend to keep seeing Jess."

"Oh, really?" Lee sneered at him. "Well, I intend to break your face!"

Jess managed to get between them again and pushed on Lee's chest. "Stop it right now! I swear to God, Lee. I'll never speak to you again if you hurt him."

He glared at Noah a few more seconds before looking down at her. "A little confused about where your loyalties should lie, Mrs. Cassady?"

She could tell he was furious, but she could also see that he was hurt. Well, she certainly knew how that felt, didn't she? Even though she hated the betrayed look she saw in Lee's eyes, she wasn't going to let him hurt Noah.

"No, Lee. My loyalty belongs with someone I trust, and that's not you anymore."

The muscles in his jaw twitched as he continued to stare at her, then he took her hands from his chest and backed away. "Fine. But if this is something you cooked up just to make me mad so I'd sign the divorce papers, it's not gonna work. And I know you, Jess. You might go out with this jerk and be willing to fight his battles for him, but you'd never sleep with him while you're still married to me."

"Go away, Lee," she said. "Don't you have an important phone call to take?"

He laughed unpleasantly and looked at Noah. "You're wasting your time, buddy. She'll never love anybody but me, no matter what she says." He started to walk away but stopped and turned back again. "Maybe I'll see you around town somewhere."

"Ignore him, Noah," Jess said. "He just likes to hear himself talk."

Noah was considerably paler than he'd been when the night had begun, and he didn't take his eyes off Lee until he'd gotten into the Mustang and backed down the driveway.

"Jess, I…" He looked at his shoes and cleared his throat. "I'm sorry."

"You have nothing to be sorry for." She took both his hands in hers. "I'm the one who should apologize for having a psychotic husband."

"I can't say I blame him for being mad. If you were my wife…" He paused to sigh. "I mean, no one would like seeing his wife with another man."

"Don't defend him, Noah. We'd be divorced already if he weren't dragging his feet. And there's no excuse for threatening you." She touched his cheek. "Are you all right?"

He nodded but didn't meet her gaze. "I'm fine, but I think it'd be best if I left now."

She sighed. "Well, I had a wonderful time tonight until this happened. Thank you for taking me." She tiptoed to kiss him, but he drew away.

"Goodnight, Jess. I'll call you tomorrow."

She watched him leave and wondered if she'd ever hear from him again.

Chapter Nine

Jess was startled awake around two-thirty by the doorbell's continuous ringing and someone pounding on her front door. When she got to the hall, she knew who it was.

"You got five seconds to let me in!" Lee shouted through the door. "Then I'm kicking in the damn door! And you know I can do it!"

"Lee, stop yelling or I'll call the police. I'm coming, you lunatic."

As soon as she unlocked it, he pushed the door open and stormed past her in a whiskey-laden cloud. "This is *my* house, dammit! I can come in any damn time I want to!"

Jess shut the door and followed him into the living room. "I can't believe you drove here this way. You could've killed yourself and other people too, you idiot."

He turned and grabbed her around the waist. "Oh, but I *didn't* drive, Mrs. Cassady. I took a cab. One more thing Miss Smarty Pants is wrong about. R-O-N-G *wrong*."

She averted her face from his alcohol-soaked breath. "That doesn't explain why you're here drunk in the middle of the night. What's the matter with you?"

"What the hell do you *think* is the matter with me? My wife's been running around behind my back with some wimpy-ass speechmaker, and she..." His expression went quickly from enraged to despondent. "You took up for him over *me*, Jess. And you won't let me come home no matter how many times I tell you I'm sorry."

His hold on her slackened along with his fading anger, so she disengaged herself from his arms. "I didn't do anything behind your back, and he has nothing to do with the divorce. I swear, I don't know if you're this clueless because you don't pay attention or if you're just plain stupid."

"It's that one, Jess—the stupid one." He tried to catch one of her hands, but he stumbled and almost fell. "I don't know what you want me to do, baby. Why won't you just tell me what to do and let me come home?"

She walked away in disgust and sat on the couch. "Well, I'm definitely not going to waste my breath explaining anything to you now when you're too drunk to even stand up. This is so immature, Lee. I can't believe you."

"I know, Jess. I'm stupid and immature without you." He fell against her as he sat down and leaned his head against her shoulder. "I need you, Jessy. You know how much I need you."

She had to struggle hard against the overwhelming weakness for him she'd always had, and she ordered herself not to feel sorry for him. All this was *his* fault and not hers, damn it.

"I know you need a swift kick in the butt for doing this, and—oh, God—I know you really need to brush your teeth." She shoved him off her shoulder and pushed him until he was lying back on the couch.

"Unfortunately, I also know you have no business being anywhere out in public like this, so just go to sleep. I'll talk to you in the morning."

He closed his eyes and nodded. "Okay, Jessy. I'll do whatever you tell me to do."

She stood there looking at him a few more seconds and had to remind herself that she was furious with him. No matter how hard she tried, she couldn't deny the maddening happiness she felt to know that he *did* care if she went out with another man. She also couldn't help feeling glad to see that he really was miserable without her.

She sighed and covered him with the chenille throw from the back of the couch before going back to her bedroom, stopping to lock the door in case he woke up and became amorously ambitious. The truth was she wasn't sure she trusted herself to resist him any more than she trusted him not to try.

She got back into bed with her mind and heart more confused than ever. If it still mattered to her so much for Lee to care about what she was doing, then she needed to take a long hard look at what she wanted to come from all this. It wasn't fair to either of them or to Noah—if she ever saw him again—to keep insisting that she wanted a divorce if all she really wanted was for Lee to convince her that he loved her enough to make her take him back.

She fell asleep and dreamed he was making love to her on the beach in St. Augustine where they'd gone for their honeymoon. Every movement and touch was so incredibly real that she woke flushed and breathless with his name on her lips. She reached for him beside her, then she cried herself back to sleep against his pillow.

****

Lee was still asleep when she got up in the morning, sprawled on the couch the way he'd taken a nap there so many times in the past. She couldn't resist stopping to look at him on her way to the kitchen and had to marvel at how, even while in dire need of a shave, his hair a mass of blond chaos and his bottom lip vibrating rather obscenely every time he exhaled, he was still the best-looking man she had ever seen. Her gaze was drawn to the way his biceps flexed on the arm bent over his head and the glorious shape of his lower body inside his wrinkled cotton pants, and her pulse quickened the way it had always done when she looked at him. God, she was so hooked on him it was like having a chemical dependency—addicted to the hormonal rush her body experienced anytime it was near his. She was nothing but a pathetic Lee junkie.

She forced herself to stop drooling over him and went into the kitchen, trying to be quiet while she made coffee. A few minutes later, an agonized groan from the living room told her he was awake. He staggered into the kitchen, scratching his head and a few other places while squinting at the coffee pot.

"How can anything that tastes so awful smell so good? You think it'll get this guy with the sledgehammer out of my head if I drink some of that nasty stuff?"

She shrugged. "Never having been stupid enough to give myself a hangover, I wouldn't know. But I guess it's worth a try."

He sat at the table and held his head in both hands. "Fix me a cup, baby."

So much for her penitent husband from the night before.

"Sure, Lee. I'll even do my best to resist dumping it on your head." She poured him a cup and set it on the table in front of him. "Here, extra cream and sugar, just the way children like it."

He picked it up with shaky hands and took a wary sip, then a bigger one. "It's not as bad as the last time I tried it. And this hangover is your fault, Jess. I hope you know that."

"I didn't tell you to get drunk, stupid."

"No, but you're the reason I had to drink the hard stuff since I was trying to forget the sight of my wife holding hands with some jerk in front of God, the neighbors, and everybody. It took a lot more than beer to get that picture out of my head."

"Poor baby," she said. "At least you don't have to live with the image of your husband screwing some bimbo."

He held his head again. "Don't yell at me, Jess. And I told you that never happened. I had to see you and Lecture Boy with my own eyes."

"You wouldn't have seen anything if you hadn't shown up here uninvited. What were you doing here anyway?"

He took a swig of coffee and set down the cup, then he reached across the table for her hand. "I came to see you as soon as I got back from New York because I couldn't wait to tell you what happened."

"I'm not interested in the highlights of how you wined and dined your way to a better job."

"No, but would you like to hear about how I convinced them to offer you a job too?"

"You did *what*?"

He smiled and rubbed the back of her hand with his thumb. "I told them I was a package deal with my wife, so if they wanted me, they had to hire you as a copyeditor."

She was so astounded for a moment that she couldn't do anything but stare at him. He clearly expected her to be happy about what he thought was such a magnanimous gesture on his part, and she supposed she should be a little encouraged by the thought and effort he must have put into it. But she would rather work on a chain gang than move to New York and edit sportswriting exclusively, and he didn't even know her well enough to realize it.

"Lee, why would you do something like that without talking to me first?"

"I didn't have time, baby. I got the idea while I was in my hotel room Friday night before the interview. I was trying to watch the Braves on TV, but all I could think about was us, trying to figure out why you wouldn't want me to get such a great job and why the hell you'd ever think you're not important to me. The only thing that made any sense was that you must not want to give up your job at the paper to go with me to New York. I called to talk to you about it, but I guess that's when you were out on your stupid dinner date."

"Lee—"

"Let me finish, Jess." He looked at her hand still clasped in his on the table. "I told the people at *Sports Spotlight* that you're the reason behind everything I've accomplished so far, so they'd be crazy not to want you on their staff. I know I was taking a big chance by making demands when they haven't even hired me yet, but I did it because I wanted you to see how important you are to me. I did it for *us*, baby. So you'd stop all this crazy divorce talk and let us get back to our life together."

He looked at her earnestly, so unaware of how far off track he was that it was almost funny. She couldn't bring herself to be mad at him when he'd honestly tried to understand and so clearly thought he was doing what she wanted, but she also couldn't let him go on thinking that he'd succeeded when he still had it so very wrong.

"Lee, I know you thought you were doing the right thing, and it means a lot to me that you even tried. It makes me want to think there's hope for us, but you still don't get what I've been trying to tell you. I've never doubted that you appreciate my help with your writing. That has nothing to do with anything."

"But, Jess—"

"No, you let me finish this time." She took a deep breath and tried to find the right words that would make him understand. "I think it's time we admitted that we didn't get married for the right reasons. I fell for you because you're so damn good-looking and I get struck with temporary insanity whenever I'm around you, and I got your attention by stroking your ego and making you dependent on me for help with your writing. I convinced myself that you wouldn't always be so wrapped up in yourself and love me only for what I could do for you. I tried to believe you'd care about me and my goals someday, but you haven't. We've been together for eight years, and you still have no idea who I am or what I want."

He looked genuinely baffled. "Jess, what are you talking about? You know I care about you."

She pulled her hand from his. "Do you really think my life's ambition is to be a copyeditor? That I don't have any goals of my own and live only to help you reach yours?"

His expression became even more confused. "What kind of goals do you mean?"

"Did you know I write short stories, Lee? Have you ever once bothered to ask me what I was doing when you got up at night and saw me at the computer?"

"I…" He ran his fingers through his hair. "I just figured you were editing."

"Why would you think that? You know I never work on anything for the paper at home except your articles, and we always do that together. No, the truth is you just didn't care what I was doing if it had nothing to do with you."

"You're not being fair, Jess. How was I supposed to know you wanted to write?"

She hadn't been angry until then, but his defensiveness was starting to irritate her. "How did I know what you wanted when we met, Lee? How did I know you hated it when people assumed you were dumb just because you're an athlete, and how much you wanted to be taken seriously as a journalist and not just a good-looking ex-jock? How did I figure out all those things without anyone telling me? By paying attention to every single thing you said and did, *that's* how."

"Okay, fine." He leaned forward with his hands on the table. "Then I have a question for you, Jess. If you know so damn much about me, then you should know this job is what I've always wanted, so why don't you want me to take it?"

She stood up and put her face right in front of his.

"I never said I didn't want you to take the damn job! I just didn't want you to take the phone call about it while you were in the middle of promising you wouldn't hurt me anymore!"

He sighed and stared into his coffee cup. "Okay, you're right. That was a stupid thing to do, but it doesn't mean I don't love you."

"I'm sure you think you love me, but I can't help wondering if you're just afraid you can't succeed without my help."

He looked up at her again. "What the hell do you want me to do? I guess I'm just too damn stupid to figure it out by myself, so just tell me."

She sat down and took a few fortifying breaths while she chose her words, because she sensed that it would be the telling moment for both of them. This was definitely the most effort he'd ever put into understanding what she needed from him. If he didn't get it now, he probably wouldn't ever get it.

"Lee, I want to be just as important to you as you've always been to me. I want you to care enough about what I think to discuss things with me, especially major issues in our lives. And I want you to share some of my interests instead of ignoring everything that doesn't pertain to you. I don't think that's too much to ask for from the man who claims to love me, and I'm tired of settling for anything less. I can't stand it when things aren't equal and balanced, and if there can't be symmetry in our marriage—equal give and take—then we shouldn't be married."

He folded his arms and leaned back to stare at her a moment. "Symmetry, huh? Sounds like some of that psycho crap you got out of that book about pulling your hair."

"No, it's something that's always been important to me. I'd think my husband would know that."

He pushed the coffee cup away from him. "And I suppose your new boyfriend is Mr. Sensitive, huh? I never knew you had a secret thing for girly men."

Her eyes narrowed as her anger flared again. "Oh, I'm sure you didn't realize I even knew there were other men in the world besides you. Right, Lee? It must've been a pretty big shock for you. No wonder you had to go out and get drunk."

"Cute, Jess. Okay, so now you've made your point. If I pretend to care about stuff like the opera and flowers and promise to pay more attention to you from now on, can I come back home?"

"God, why do I even bother?" She threw up her hands and looked at the ceiling before standing. "I'm going to take a shower. Help yourself to more coffee, then get out."

"Jess, wait. We need to talk some more."

She ignored him and walked out of the kitchen. She'd spelled it out for him as plainly as she could, and he was still as clueless as ever. Apparently, he didn't want to get it.

She got in the shower and turned on the water full blast the way she liked it, letting the deluge carry away her bitter tears.

Chapter Ten

Lee was gone when she got out of the shower. She found a note taped to her computer monitor that said he would give her a few days to get over being mad before they finished their conversation, but she should call him if she needed somebody to hold her hand or buy her dinner.

She turned on the answering machine so she wouldn't be disturbed and spent the day reading posts in an online forum for people with TTM—"trichsters" as they called themselves. She enjoyed the camaraderie and exchange of ideas with people going through the same things she was dealing with, and since it also seemed as if most of the other members were suffering a lot more than she was from the illness, it tended to make her own problems seem much less severe in comparison.

However, one thing that bothered her was a prevailing attitude of self-loathing and recrimination in many of the other members. Some of them seemed to feel they were flawed, crazy, weak, or otherwise unworthy of feeling normal because they had TTM, as if they deserved to be miserable because it stemmed from a character defect.

Jess was particularly affected by a sixteen-year-old girl named Cara who had dropped out of school because she lived in fear of anyone finding out she wore a wig to hide her bald spots. Cara had posted about how she'd never had a boyfriend because of her self-esteem issues and rarely left her house anymore, even though her profile showed a pretty girl who reminded Jess of Lee's younger sister, Lexie. Cara said her parents thought she was crazy and had given up on her after sending her to three different doctors, none of whom had ever heard of TTM. The last one had referred her to a psychiatrist and had even suggested institutionalization.

It broke Jess's heart to read her posts. She e-mailed Cara privately to offer a sympathetic ear anytime she needed it and got a response immediately. Jess could tell how lonely the poor girl was. She was delighted to discover that Cara liked to write poetry and hoped to publish it someday, so they were able to share their creative aspirations with each other.

Over the next couple of weeks, they corresponded daily by e-mail. The encouragement and support she was able to give Cara helped Jess improve her own state of mind and also helped her regain the independent mindset she had achieved in the weeks prior to the night she'd gone to Noah's lecture.

Just as she'd feared, she hadn't heard from Noah since the night of the play. She thought about calling or going to his apartment, but what could she say to him? Since she wasn't sure she could offer him the kind of relationship he was hoping for and didn't want to mislead him, she thought maybe it was better that he'd decided to stay away.

For a while, Lee had called her every night, probably just to make sure she wasn't out on any more dates. But after two weeks passed and he found out she hadn't heard from Noah, he evidently decided he had scared away the competition and went back to his career planning. Jess kept expecting to hear an announcement at work that he'd been hired by *Sports Spotlight*, but none had materialized so far.

Ever since Marjorie's disastrous visit, Jess hadn't done more than say hello to her mother when she called home. She could be just as stubborn as her mother, so Jess refused to apologize or try to make amends. Her father had been a little more sympathetic when she'd talked to him about the divorce, but he still claimed to agree with Marjorie as he usually did. Jess knew it was probably for the sake of his own peace, but she couldn't help wishing he'd stand up to Marjorie for once and be on his daughter's side. When she called him on Father's Day, she got another not-so-subtle admonition from him.

"Don't worry about not making it home, Jess," Bill said. "I'd much rather have you there working on your marriage. Resolving your problems with Lee would be the best gift you could give me."

"I'm sorry, Daddy, but that's not going to happen. Some problems are insurmountable."

"That's only true in the case of physical abuse, criminal activity, and political affiliation, honey. Everything else should be negotiable."

"Very funny, Daddy. I guess I'm just not as willing to overlook things as you've always been."

"You have to pick your battles, sweetheart. Prioritize and mediate—that's always worked for me. At the office and at home."

Jess didn't bother pointing out how much he stayed at the office and volunteered for overtime, even though he could have retired five years earlier. She promised she'd make it home to Tampa for a visit soon and hung up before he had the chance to ask if she wanted to speak to her mother.

When she checked her e-mail, she found a heart-wrenching message from Cara saying her dad had told her the only Father's Day gift he wanted was a normal daughter. Cara sounded so despondent that Jess feared she was becoming suicidal. She didn't know what Cara was doing to control her hair-pulling and didn't feel qualified to suggest treatment to anyone, but she decided to take a chance and tell her about the treatment plan in *The Hair-Pulling Problem*. Jess was surprised to find that Cara had never heard of it before.

Cara begged Jess to coach her on how to do it since she knew her parents wouldn't buy the book for her, and she had no money of her own. Jess explained it the best she could, and Cara wrote back that it gave her a reason to go on and she could finally imagine a real future for herself.

Jess was in tears at knowing she'd been able to make such a difference in someone's life. Lee called as she was reading Cara's message, and she tried not to let him know she was crying. Just her luck, he picked then to be perceptive.

"What's wrong, Jess? Have you been talking to your mother again?"

"No. It's nothing. What are you calling about?"

"Don't give me that. I can tell you're upset about something. What's wrong, baby?"

His unexpected sensitivity got to her. It also made her realize just how frightened she'd been that Cara would do something desperate, and she welcomed the chance to confide in someone. She told him all about Cara, and he didn't say anything for a few seconds when she finished. While she was bracing herself for one of his callous remarks that would make her regret telling him, he surprised her again.

"You did the right thing, Jess. In fact, you probably saved her life. She sounds just like Lexie before she tried to kill herself last year."

Jess knew Lexie had been struggling with depression ever since their father's death, but Lee had never said anything about a suicide attempt.

"Oh my God, Lee." Jess fell onto the sofa with her hand over her mouth. "Why didn't you tell me?"

"She promised Mom and me that it wouldn't happen again and begged us not to tell anybody. I didn't want to keep it from you, Jess, but her doctor said it had to be Lexie's decision to tell anybody about her illness."

"What illness?"

He hesitated a moment. "If I tell you, will you give me credit for trusting you over everybody else?"

"Lee, stop thinking about earning brownie points and tell me about Lexie."

He sighed, then he said, "She has severe OCD—Obsessive Compulsive Disorder. Her doctor's tried her on tons of different drugs, and Prozac seems to work the best for her. She's been doing a lot better since she went on it after the suicide attempt."

Lexie's unease around strangers and a few other odd habits Jess had always attributed to shyness and teenage awkwardness suddenly made sense in light of Lee's revelation. Jess had always loved her young sister-in-law, and finding all this out made her want to cry.

"Lee, OCD and my hair-pulling are related disorders. I've been reading a lot about them both lately. Do you think she'd want to talk to me about it if she knew why I understand what she's going through?"

"You don't have to do that, Jess. You're already helping this other girl. That's enough for you to worry about."

"Don't be silly, Lee. You know I love Lexie. If I can help her at all, it'll help me too."

He was quiet for a couple of seconds, then he said, "Damn it, Jess! This is just more proof that we're supposed to be together. Can't you see that?"

"No, I can see it's more proof that you think everything is about *you,* but I don't want to fight with you about it now. I'm more concerned about Lexie. Will you ask her and your mom if I can come over and talk to them?"

He sighed. "Yeah, you know I will."

"Good. Now what were you calling me about in the first place?"

"Never mind." His voice sounded odd. "You've got your hands full already."

"You know it drives me crazy when you do that. What did you want?"

"No, it'll just make you mad at me again."

"I promise I won't get mad, Lee. Just tell me."

He sighed again. "I called to see if you'd go with me to put flowers on my dad's grave. I know I'm probably being selfish again, but I didn't want to go by myself. It's okay if you don't want to do it."

"Of course I'll go with you. Do you want me to meet you there?"

"No, I'll pick you up. I kinda need you to help me pick out the flowers first."

She had to smile. "Okay, I'll be ready when you get here."

She knew it was very possible that Lee had asked her to go with him just to draw her sympathy, but she had loved Hal Cassady like a father herself and was glad for the chance to honor his memory. He'd been such a generous, big-hearted man who had worked so hard all his life, and he'd made Jess feel like a part of their family from the first time she'd met him.

When Lee picked her up, they drove to a roadside stand where Jess helped him select a mixed bouquet of wildflowers, their simple beauty fitting for a down-to-earth man like Hal had been. Lee made no effort to hide his tears when he placed the flowers on his father's grave, and Jess had to wipe hers away as well. He took her hand when they started back to the car, and she was glad to let him hold it.

When they got back to the house and Lee parked in the driveway, he shut off the engine and took her hand again. "Thanks for going with me, Jess. Dad always loved you, so I know he's happy you were there with me."

"Thank you for asking me to go, Lee. I loved your dad too."

He lowered his gaze. "I miss him like hell, but I'm kinda glad I don't have to face him right now and explain why I've screwed up my marriage and haven't accomplished anything he could be proud of."

"That's not true," she said. "Your dad was always proud of you."

He shook his head. "I know how disappointed he

was when I had to quit playing football. I thought if I could hit it big as a sportswriter, it would make it up to him a little."

So that was why he was so driven to succeed. Why hadn't she ever realized it before?

"Your dad just wanted you to be happy, Lee. He was upset about your knee injury because he knew how much you loved playing, not because he wanted you to become rich or famous."

"No, he told me when I was in high school that he didn't want me to have to work myself to death just to provide for my family the way he did."

"That's right. He didn't want you doing manual labor in a factory like him, and you accomplished that by going to college. He was proud of you for getting your degree, but I think he was even more proud of you for being such a devoted son and brother."

He looked up at her. "You sound like my mom. I know you're both just trying to make me feel better."

"That's ridiculous." She pushed his shoulder. "Neither one of us even likes you."

His smile made her heart beat erratically. "I'm trying to understand what you want me to do so I can come home, Jess. I swear I am."

"I believe you, Lee. To tell the truth, I'm not even sure *I* know what I want you to do. I just know I want things to be different."

"Today was a good start, wasn't it?"

"Yeah, it was," she said and meant it.

He squeezed her hand. "I want to do something special for you like you did for me today. Whatever you want. Just tell me."

"You don't need to repay me for anything. I was

glad to go with you."

"No, there's gotta be something I can do. Think about it and let me know, okay?"

"Okay, I'll think about it."

"Jess…" He twisted his wedding ring on his finger. "Please don't go out with that guy if he starts calling you again. I know you wouldn't sleep with him, but I can't stand the idea of him even touching you."

She sighed. "I don't think that's an issue anymore. I'm sure he wants to stay as far away from me as possible now that he knows I have a violent lunatic for a husband." His face flooded with relief, but she couldn't quite seem to get mad at him for it.

"I guess he got a look at these pythons, huh?" He flexed his biceps for her. "Decided he'd better find his own woman and leave mine alone."

She arched an eyebrow. "You've been watching wrestling with Trent, haven't you?"

He gave her another of his heart-stopping smiles and leaned over to kiss her on the cheek. She was thankful it was only a chaste kiss, because she wasn't sure she could have resisted him if he'd tried to kiss her for real. Just the brush of his lips on her face was an exquisite agony she knew all too well.

Sensing that she needed to put some space between them, she opened the car door and said, "I'll see you at work tomorrow, Lee. Don't forget to ask your mom about letting me come over to see Lexie."

"Okay, I will. Don't forget I love you, Jess."

Once she was safely inside the house, she fell onto the couch and listened to the sound of his car pulling away, nearly in a panic at the realization that she was always going to love a man who hurt her on a regular basis and would likely keep doing so, because he did it unintentionally. And the thing that scared her the most was knowing she would probably end up sacrificing everything else that was important to her and let him go on hurting her, because the times in between the pain were the moments she lived for.

Chapter Eleven

After an hour spent lying on her bed wondering what to do about the mess she'd made of her life and berating herself for it, Jess decided to call her best friend so she could cheer her up. She was also counting on Deb to talk her out of doing anything drastic—like calling off the divorce first thing in the morning and seducing Lee on the notorious conference table at work.

"Okay, listen to me closely," Deb said after hearing the details of Jess's afternoon with Lee. "Let's break this down rationally into pros and cons. On the pro side, you really do love the jerk and you want to jump his bones even when he looks like a homeless wino. On the con side, you're tired of babying him and pretending you don't have a life or a mind of your own. So why can't you go ahead with the divorce and just let him drop by every Friday night to do the wild thang with you?"

Jess laughed, feeling better already. "Oh, sure. Why didn't I think of that before?"

"Beats me. It's pretty cut and dry from where I sit."

"Well, your solution might not be feasible, but your analysis is dead-on. I'm just not sure which way I'd be more miserable—with him or without him."

"Well, what's the big freaking rush in making up your mind, Jess? You said he really seems to be trying right now, so just let him keep at it. My guess is he'll either finally get it right or bury himself, with odds in favor of the latter."

"I know, but it feels dishonest to keep insisting that I want a divorce when I don't think I do anymore. Or that I ever really did." Jess switched the phone to her other hand and lifted Ming onto her lap. "I mean, it's not like Lee has ever done anything cruel or disrespectful to me, and I know he'd never hurt me intentionally."

"Yeah, but do you think he'll ever get enough of a clue to quit stomping all over your feelings every time he turns around?"

"I don't know. I believe he's trying right now, but it could just be that seeing me with Noah threatened his masculinity and has him on the defensive." Jess sighed and scratched Ming under the chin. "I hate people who play emotional games, and that's what it feels like I'm doing. I feel like such a hypocrite."

"No, sweetie," Deb said. "You're not one of those people. In typical Jess fashion, you're reevaluating and reorganizing your life, and it's just taking you a while to do it. That's all."

"I love you, Deb. I don't think I tell you that enough."

"Yeah, I know. I'll remind you the next time we go shopping together in Atlanta. You can profess your love by getting me that little backless number we saw at Macy's."

****

The next morning, Lee told Jess he'd talked to his mother and gotten the okay for her to come over when she got off that afternoon. On the drive to their house, Jess chided herself again for not noticing his sister's problems before. There'd been a few times in the past when she'd noticed that Lexie sometimes repeated things, but it hadn't registered as a real problem. And she knew Lexie didn't drive, but she'd always chalked it up to a personality quirk. Here she was always complaining about Lee's selfishness, but how self-absorbed was she herself not to have seen what Lexie was going through? Well, she planned to make up for it now.

Sharon Cassady greeted Jess as always with a warm hug. "It's so good to see you again, sweetie. I've missed you coming over with Lee the last few times, but I know you've been busy. He says the paper has you working so many extra hours because you're the best copyeditor they have."

"Well, you know Lee tends to exaggerate," Jess said. "But I've missed you too, Mrs. C."

Sharon's blue eyes—so much like Lee's—looked at Jess earnestly. "I'm sorry we didn't tell you about Lexie before, but—"

"It's okay. Lee explained it to me. I just hope she's not upset that he told me now."

Sharon patted her arm. "Don't worry. She was a little put out with him at first, but when he told her you knew all about OCD and were even dealing with something similar, she was excited about the prospect of talking to you about it. Thank you for taking the time to come see her."

Jess smiled. "If I can help her even a little, it'll be like therapy for me. Lexie's the little sister I always wanted but never got."

Sharon hugged her again. "I'm so glad Lee has you. You're the only one besides his father who can keep him grounded. I think that's a big part of why Hal loved you so much."

"Thank you, Mrs. C. I loved him too."

Jess felt a pang of guilt at the thought of how upset this sweet woman would be if she knew about their marriage problems. Still, as she followed his mother down the hall to Lexie's room, she couldn't help wondering if Lee had been feigning his initial reluctance at her coming over here. He had to know how deeply this visit with his family would affect her and was probably hoping it would help his case. She might have resolved herself to always being in love with the jerk, but that didn't mean she wasn't on to him.

Sharon knocked on Lexie's door and leaned in when she opened it. "Honey, Jess is here to see you. I'll be in the kitchen if either of you need me."

Jess went in and scanned the newly painted walls. "Wow, Lex. I really like what you've done to your room."

"Thanks," Lexie said. "I forgot you haven't seen it since I painted. Lee told us how busy your job has been keeping you."

With another twinge of guilt over her deception, Jess moved the chair from the dresser over beside the bed and sat down facing Lexie. "He told you why I wanted to see you today too, didn't he?"

Lexie nodded and tucked a lock of blonde hair behind her ear. "I know he told you about my OCD. I'm sorry I wouldn't let him tell you about it before, but I used to be pretty paranoid about anyone finding out about it."

"It's okay. I understand why you wanted it kept quiet. I'm just glad you don't mind my knowing about it now."

"To tell the truth, I'm surprised you knew what he was talking about. People with OCD usually get looked at like they're a loony-tune when they talk about it."

"Well, you're not loony and I'm not most people. As a matter of fact, you could say I have something a little like OCD myself."

Lexie tucked her feet under her to sit cross-legged. "How do you mean?"

Jess glanced at Lexie's dresser covered with a huge assortment of fashion jewelry that was so unusual she had to ask about it. "These are beautiful, Lex. Where in the world did you get them?"

"*Jess*," Lexie repeated a little impatiently. "What do you mean you have something like OCD?"

"Oh, sorry. I mean I have trichotillomania. Have you ever heard of it?"

"I'm not sure. Lee said something about you pulling your hair sometimes, but he said he'd let you explain it to me so he wouldn't mess it up."

"Good thing." Jess smiled at the thought of how Lee would have mangled the explanation. "It's a condition that causes people to pull out their hair or eyebrows or lashes in an effort to restore balance to their nervous systems. Like OCD, it's influenced by a lack of serotonin in the brain. And I'm lucky that I don't suffer from the terrible anxiety you feel from what you think might happen if you don't comply with your compulsions."

"You really do understand, Jess!" Lexie sprang up from the bed and wrapped her arms around Jess's neck. "I'm so glad Lee told you!"

"Me too, Lex." Jess clasped her hand around

Lexie's head, snuggling her deeper into the hug.

Lexie sat on the edge of the bed again, her eyes on Jess's thick auburn hair. "But you don't have any bald spots or anything. I remember seeing a girl on *Oprah* once who had to wear a wig because she pulled out almost all her hair. I think she was supposed to have the same thing you have."

"Well, thank God for thick hair, and for the book I found about it," Jess said. "It's really helping me. But you're right about the girl you saw. Usually the only people the public ever hears about are the extreme cases."

Lexie nodded. "How long have you had it?"

"I'm not really sure. Always I suppose, but I guess the things that triggered it didn't surface until adulthood. I know stress makes it harder to manage, so that could've been the catalyst that started it." She hoped Lexie wouldn't ask about the main source of her stress, because she didn't want to tell her it was her beloved big brother. She reached over and covered Lexie's hand with hers. "How have you been doing with your treatment?"

"The Prozac my doctor prescribed is helping me a lot," Lexie said, "but I can't tell you how many times I've wished I had someone I could talk to that really understands how I feel. I know I have Mama and Lee, but it's not the same thing. They've never had to deal with the craziness that goes on in my head sometimes."

Jess smoothed a stray lock of hair from Lexie's forehead. "What about counseling? Lee said you've been seeing a psychiatrist. How's that going?"

"Oh, fine I guess." Lexie pulled her legs up to sit cross-legged on the bed. "I love Dr. Hart and think she's a great doctor, but she doesn't have OCD herself. Everything she knows about my illness came from studying it in doctor books. She doesn't live with it day in and day out. That's why I'm so glad to finally know someone else who has OCD, even if it's just a little bit."

"Well, mine is different from OCD, but my hair pulling probably puts me closer to understanding your situation than most people. I'm glad Lee confided in me."

"Me too," Lexie said. "And I know what you mean about stress being a trigger. When Daddy died, I thought I would completely lose my mind. My repeating got so bad that Mama says she once counted to two hundred and three before I finally let her stop answering me."

Jess's eyes grew wide. "You've made your mother repeat phrases back to you into the hundreds before?"

"Yep. The books don't tell you that, huh? They say 'people with OCD tend to repeat things…blah, blah, blah.' They don't really scratch the surface of the reality of this illness, and it's not even always the same. I've had periods where I do everything in odd numbers, and I don't know why I like multiples of three, but I just do. I may do something nine times or I may have to do it a hundred and ninety-three times before my anxiety about it is satisfied. It's a wonder I haven't driven Mama crazy by now."

Jess held back the tears that threatened as she sat beside Lexie on the bed. "What's your earliest memory of having it?"

Lexie answered without hesitation. "I was seven years old and was the flower girl in my cousin's wedding. You know how you have to carry the basket and drop the rose petals down the aisle? Well, just as I started down the aisle, I accidentally dropped the basket and spilled almost all the petals in one spot. I hurried and scooped it up, then for some reason I had to drop it three more times before I could make it down the aisle." She paused for an awkward laugh. "It's a little funny now, but the bride sure didn't think so then. She shot daggers at me every time that little white basket hit the floor, I can tell you that."

Jess's eyebrow rose in amusement. If Elise's flower girl had dropped the basket of flowers even once, Marjorie would've been the one shooting weapons from her eye sockets, and the poor child's life would have been in danger from that insufferable wedding planner.

"Why did you keep dropping it, Lex?"

"I didn't know. All I knew was that I was doing it on purpose and couldn't stop myself, even though I didn't know why I was doing it. Now I know it was my OCD. I guess it was the beginning of many scattered rose petals for me."

A shiver tickled Jess's spine at the poignancy of her words.

"Actually, Dr. Hart thinks it's possible I wasn't born with OCD," Lexie added.

"Really? What does she think caused it?"

"I had a really bad case of scarlet fever when I was four, and some doctors think it can cause OCD in rare cases because it depletes the brain of serotonin and changes the way it's stored. But I guess we'll never know what truly caused it. Kinda weird, huh?"

"Not weird, just unusual," Jess said. "But you seem

to be making wonderful progress and have a good perspective about it all. I mean, when Lee told me about the—" She stopped, unsure if she should mention the suicide attempt.

"It's okay, Jess." Lexie's smile relieved the awkwardness of the moment. "Lee told you I tried to kill myself after Daddy died, right?"

"Yes, but only because he knows I understand why."

"Like I said, I thought I'd lose my mind during that time. But I didn't, and I'm still here, so I guess I was stronger than all that anxiety after all, huh?"

"Yes, you most definitely are, and I'm so proud of you for it." Jess embraced her again. "Please forgive me for not knowing what was going on with you. I should've been more perceptive and done something, but I just thought you were depressed like anyone would be after the loss of a parent. If I'd had an idea—"

"You would've done what?" Lexie asked. "There was nothing anyone could do for me at that time, Jess. The fact is I have OCD, and everything I've had to go through has brought me closer to understanding my illness and learning how to live with it—even the suicide attempt served a purpose, because now I can recognize the signs if I start to feel that way again and tell my doctor about it before it gets worse."

Jess's eyes filled with tears. "Do you have any idea how incredible it is that you can deal with this so well?"

"It's all I know, Jess. I think one of the biggest reasons I'm doing better now is that I haven't just accepted my illness, I've embraced it. It's part of who I am, and as crazy as it sounds, I think I'd be afraid *not* to have OCD, because I don't know who I'd be without it.

Besides, I kinda like who I am, you know? It took me awhile to realize that, but I finally did."

How could this teenager have such personal insight and strong will at such a young age? Jess had come to offer Lexie support and help her know she wasn't alone, but Lexie was turning out to be the inspirational one.

"I'm glad you like who you are, Lex, because you're amazing."

"Thanks, Jess. So have you embraced your hair pulling yet?"

Jess wasn't sure she'd embraced it, but she felt as if she'd accepted it. She just wished her mother could accept it or at least acknowledge that her daughter even had an illness.

"I'm controlling it. Most of the time anyway."

"Good. And I'm glad you finally know what's been going on with me. I still have good days and bad days, but—"

"Don't we all?" Jess said as Lee's face appeared in her mind.

Lexie nodded. "But it's good to know I have you to talk to now if I have a bad day."

"Good, because you do, Lex. Call me anytime you need to talk."

Jess gave her another hug. The honesty and emotion coming from Lexie was the sweetest thing she'd experienced in a long time. When she got up to replace the chair at the dresser, her attention was again drawn to the jewelry spread out over it.

"I love your jewelry," Jess said. "It's so beautiful."

"Thanks. I make it."

Surprise lit Jess's eyes. "Really? I knew you were

creative and artistic, but I had no idea you were this talented." She peered inside a couple of the boxes on the floor beside the dresser. Each one was filled with hundreds of glass beads and colored stones.

"It's one of the only up-sides to having OCD," Lexie said. "I have mountains of patience and can sit and work for hours until each piece is absolutely perfect. And I love sorting through the beads for hours—the more tedious the better. It makes me feel such control and gratification when I finish a piece."

"I know exactly what you mean, Lex. There are some things I think I do especially well because I have TTM, like spotting typos when I'm editing." Jess held up a bracelet made of an odd but beautiful type of crystal. "What's this one called?"

"Aurora borealis. Beautiful, aren't they?"

"Gorgeous." Jess admired the myriad colors of the crystals. "Lex, you could sell this jewelry."

Lexie fingered the items on the dresser. "Sure, if I could ever muster the courage to mingle with people again during the day instead of sleeping through it."

"What do you mean?"

Lexie explained that she preferred to stay awake until the wee hours of the morning, surfing the Internet and talking to friends online. Then she'd sleep until mid-afternoon each day, because being a night owl afforded her the luxury of solitude. While the rest of the world was sleeping, she didn't have to deal with the anxiety she experienced from interaction with people and wasn't at the mercy of the constant phrase repeating that occurred when a simple comment ignited one of her triggers.

Jess couldn't help thinking what a tragedy it was

that both Lexie and Cara felt they had to hide themselves away in shame to battle illnesses that society had deemed strange without bothering to fully comprehend them. And that gave her an idea.

"Lex, there's someone I'd like you to meet if it's okay with you. She's a girl your age that I met online in a forum for people with TTM. Is it okay if I give her your e-mail address so she can write to you?"

Lexie's face showed her delight. "Sure, Jess. It would be cool to have a friend my age who understands about this stuff. Tell her to e-mail me tonight. Maybe we can IM too if she's a night owl like me."

"I'll send her a message as soon as I get home." Jess held up a cameo pin. "Oh my God. Don't tell me you made this one too."

Lexie lifted one shoulder. "Guilty."

"It's exquisite. I love it, Lex."

"Then you keep it."

"Oh, I couldn't."

"Why not?" Lexie opened a drawer, displaying dozens of other cameo pins. "I've made lots of them and could probably even teach you how to do it. Besides, I want you to have it."

"Thank you, Lex. I'll put it on right now." Jess fastened the pin to her blouse. "I'll think about you every time I wear it." She gave Lexie another hug. "It'll remind me to be strong—like you."

****

Jess drove home feeling encouraged by her visit with Lexie, and her fingers drifted to the cameo pinned to her collar. As she moved her thumb over its delicate contours, she remembered what Lexie had said about liking who she was, OCD and all. She started to feel less guilty about trying to get a divorce she'd never really wanted. Maybe all this had happened because she'd needed the time on her own to get to know herself as more than just Lee's wife.

And as Deb had pointed out, what was the hurry about letting him come back just because she knew she was always going to love him despite his faults? She definitely had his attention right now, so she might as well use this opportunity to show him she'd outgrown the one-sided relationship they'd had in the past and that her goals and interests mattered every bit as much as his.

She touched the cameo again and smiled. "See, you *do* help me to be strong."

Chapter Twelve

Jess e-mailed Cara as soon as she got home and gave her Lexie's e-mail address. She could tell from the almost immediate reply she got that Cara was just as thrilled as Lexie was over the prospect of having a friend her own age, especially one who understood what she was going through.

As Jess got ready to go to the third installment of her lecture series, her stomach fluttered at the possibility—slight though it was—of seeing Noah there, and she wasn't sure if she was hoping for it or dreading it. If she did see him there, she would have to be honest and tell him she was reconsidering the divorce, but she liked him so much that she hoped they could be friends regardless.

"You know you're a basket case, right?" she said to her reflection. "You can't make up your mind about anything, you're too much of a chicken to let anyone read your stories, and you still pull your hair when you watch TV." She paused to scowl at herself in the mirror. "And you talk to yourself."

When she turned to slip her feet into her sandals, her fingers touched the cameo pinned to her blouse. She looked at her reflection again with a little smile.

"But you *do* have beautiful feet," she said defiantly. "And your new toe ring is utterly adorable." She wiggled her toes and admired the glittering blue eyes of the Siamese cat adorning the second toe of her right foot.

When she arrived at the junior college, she scanned the parking lot but didn't see Noah's car, so she went inside with a resigned sigh. The lecture topic for the night was "Judicial Review in the New Nation," but the speaker, a visiting professor from Georgia Tech, didn't even come close to Noah's caliber. Jess found her mind drifting away from *Marbury vs. Madison* to the memory of Noah's captivating voice and sweet smile.

She wasn't moved to question the speaker about anything after the lecture and didn't linger when it ended. The moment she saw Noah standing next to her car in the parking lot, she knew without a doubt that she'd been hoping to see him all along. She hurried over to him with her hands outstretched to take his.

"Noah, I'm so glad you're here."

He took her hands and smiled. "I'm relieved to hear you say that. I was afraid you wouldn't speak to me since I've behaved so badly for the past few weeks."

"I don't blame you for avoiding me. I'm so sorry for the way Lee acted." She didn't miss the change in his expression at the mention of Lee's name.

"To be honest, I have to admit I didn't expect there to still be such strong feelings between the two of you. The things he said threw me for a loop at first, but I meant it when I told him I intended to keep seeing you. I hope you haven't changed your mind about letting me."

"I have to be honest too," she said. "I can't say I'm still as sure about the divorce as I thought I was, but I *can* say that I'd truly hate it if I couldn't see you anymore. I don't want to lose you as a friend no matter what happens."

He studied the hardtack surface of the parking lot a moment, then he looked up with a little smile. "Well, if you haven't called off the divorce yet, I suppose it means I still have a small chance of winning you over, and I'm not going to chicken out this time. I might end up with my face rearranged, but maybe it will be an improvement."

She shook her head with a rueful laugh. "I like your face just the way it is, thank you very much. And I'm not willing to give up our friendship because of Lee's macho posturing. Besides, I don't think he'd really resort to actual violence. I'm sure he'd be too worried about possibly damaging his own pretty face in the process."

"I'm very glad to hear that, on both accounts." He lowered his gaze again a moment. "I understand if you need to keep our relationship on a platonic level right now, but I was planning to ask you to go with me to view the Perseids meteor shower a week from next Friday. My stargazing club watches it together at the school system's environmental studies center every summer. Would you like to go with me?"

It sounded like a safe enough activity for them to share as friends, and Jess had always loved stargazing, another interest she and Lee didn't share. He had no patience for watching meteors and couldn't tell the Little Dipper from Orion's Belt.

"I'd love to, Noah. Thank you for asking me."

She was again struck by how much her acceptance meant to him. "Great. I'll pick you up that Friday at eleven—the shower peaks at midnight. I'll bring us a couple of lawn chairs and some snacks, and you'll probably need to wear a light jacket."

"Okay, it's a date." She saw him looking at the cameo pinned to her collar and said, "It's beautiful, isn't it?"

"Yes, and so unique. My mother has cameos, but I've never seen one like that before."

"It was handmade by my husband's younger sister, a very special young lady." Jess touched the pin fondly. "It has a deeply personal meaning for me."

"Oh. I can see how it would."

She could tell he thought she meant because of the connection to Lee, but she didn't correct him. "I'm so glad you came to see me tonight, Noah, and I'm really looking forward to our stargazing date."

He smiled and opened the car door for her. "So am I. Goodnight, Jess."

He waited by her car until she was inside with the door locked, and she knew he wouldn't leave until he'd seen her safely on her way. He was such a sweet, considerate man, so why hadn't she explained about the cameo's meaning and confided in him about her hair pulling? Evidently, she hadn't accepted her disorder as well as she thought she had if it still bothered her to admit it because someone might think she was crazy or weird.

And the funny thing was that it hadn't bothered her at all for Lee to know when her mother had told him. She hadn't worried for even a second that he would think or feel any differently about her because of it. If she'd stopped and thought about it then, she would have realized it was because she'd always known he really cared about her no matter how thoughtless and insensitive he could be at times.

She fingered the cameo and hoped it would help her in the future with courage, insight, and strength. Maybe that's what she should ask for at the meteor shower if she got the chance to wish on any shooting stars.

****

Lee was waiting for her in the hall the next morning when she and Deb got off the elevator at work.

"Jess, I need to talk to you about something," he said. "Come to the conference room with me for a minute, okay?"

Deb folded her arms and sneered at him. "What's wrong, Lee? Having trouble writing complete sentences without her?"

He glared back at her. "Hasn't anyone dropped a house on you yet?"

"You can kiss my unimpressed ass, you—"

"Stop it, both of you," Jess said. "Come on, Lee. I'll go talk to you, but I only have a couple of minutes."

"Thanks, baby." He shot Deb an unpleasant smile and put his hand on the small of Jess's back as they walked away. "It won't take long."

"Careful, Jess," Deb called after them. "Sounds like he's got sex in mind."

Jess held on to Lee's arm to keep him from turning around and whispered, "Don't say anything else. And at least that comment proves she's obviously never slept with you."

He shuddered. "Don't even joke about that." They went in the conference room, and he closed the door behind them. "Thanks for talking to me, Jess. Mom wanted me to let you know how much it meant to her for you to come over and see Lexie yesterday. They both love you as much as Dad did."

"You know I love them too, Lee."

"Yeah, I do," he said, taking her hands. "And I also know we're gonna fix things between us. I can already feel how much closer we've been lately, and I'm not gonna stop until I figure out everything I need to do."

"I've been thinking about a lot of things too," she said. "Thanks again for setting up the visit with Lexie. I think it might have helped me more than it did her."

"You're welcome, but I still want to do something special for you. Have you thought of anything yet?"

She started to tell him no, then she remembered an idea she'd gotten the night before when she'd checked her e-mail after she got home from the lecture.

"There is something you could help me with. You remember the girl named Cara that I met online? I want to give her a copy of the hair-pulling book I ordered, but I can't mail it because I won't let her give me her address. That's a dangerous online practice that I told her she can never risk, no matter how much she thinks she can trust someone."

"So how are you gonna get the book to her?"

"I know she lives near Jacksonville, and she thinks she can get her uncle to come with her to meet me somewhere nearby so I can give her a copy of the book. If you want to do something for me, you can drive me there when we get it all set up."

"Sure, no problem. Just let me know when."

"Okay. Thanks, Lee." She started to leave, but he caught her hand and pulled her back.

"I love you, Jess. Don't ever forget that."

For a second she thought he was going to kiss her,

but he only brushed her cheek with his fingertips and said he'd see her later. She stopped in the doorway to watch him walk away and realized how many times he'd told her he loved her since they'd been apart, even though she hadn't said it back to him even once since their breakup. She didn't think she could have kept saying it to someone who wouldn't reciprocate, and she had to give him credit for his unwavering belief that she loved him even when she wouldn't tell him so.

"Okay, quit staring at his ass and tell me what he wanted," Deb said when she walked up behind her.

Jess turned around with a sigh. "I really wish you two would stop with the verbal wrestling matches. It puts me in the middle and I hate it."

"Fine, I'll ignore him from now on. Now tell me what he said."

"He wants to do something special for me because I went to the cemetery with him on Father's Day. I told him he can drive me to Florida to meet Cara, the girl I met online that I told you about."

Deb looked disappointed that it wasn't something juicier. "What did he say when you told him about your stargazing date with Noah?"

That familiar knot returned to Jess's stomach.

"I…didn't tell him about that yet, but I will. If he can't be mature about it and consider my feelings, it'll be a prime example for him of what I've been trying to make him see."

They stopped by the break room for their coffee, and Deb said, "So if he blows a gasket when you tell him about the date, you think he'll go after Noah?"

"He'd better not. He knows that's something I wouldn't forgive him for."

Deb stirred her coffee with a sigh. "One of these days, you gotta tell me your secret, Jess. You've got two of them professing their undying devotion, and I can't even get Howie to move out of his mother's house."

"Well, Howie is definitely a unique case," Jess said. "But I know he's crazy about you. He'll see the light one of these days."

"Yeah, but it probably won't be until his mama is called into The Light."

****

Jess arranged to meet Cara the following weekend at the library in Clayton, a little town near Jacksonville. Lee picked her up Saturday morning at seven to make the three-hour drive. When she got in the car, he greeted her with a cup of coffee from the Java Joint and a big grin.

"See what I brought you, Jess? Am I making progress or what?"

She took the cup and removed the lid. "Lee, you've already added cream and sugar to this, and some of it's gone."

He shrugged nonchalantly as he backed down the driveway. "I just tasted it for you."

She took a sip and grimaced. "Oh, God. There's enough sugar in this to put me in a diabetic coma."

"It tasted okay to me. I'll drink it if you don't want it. No sense wasting it."

She shoved him. "You're such a liar. You bought this for yourself."

He laughed and opened the console to retrieve another cup. "Here's yours, baby. I was just jostling you."

She took the cup with a wry smile. "Joshing, Lee. And thanks."

He put his hand on her knee. "No, thank you for letting me do this for you. I hope today will make you see how important you are to me."

She concentrated on stirring her coffee and tried not to let him see how much she was hoping the same thing. "Well, I appreciate your help. Really."

"So does this girl know I'm coming with you?"

Jess nodded. "I told her it wouldn't be any safer for me to come alone than it would be for her. As much time as she spends online, she has to learn the rules and never take chances on something like this."

"Does she know I'm your husband?"

She gave him a sly look. "Why? Are you planning to hit on her?"

"If you think it would help," he said. "You know, a little flirting to boost her self-esteem?"

Jess's smile softened. "That's sweet, Lee, but she knows you're my husband. Just be nice to her."

"I'm nice to everybody, Jess. Except your friend the viper and guys who hold my wife's hand." He winced and looked at her sideways. "Ignore that. I don't want to start a fight."

"I don't want to fight either, so let's stay away from the touchy subjects, okay?" She still intended to tell him about her date with Noah, but she didn't want tension between them all day and had decided to wait and tell him when they got back.

"So I guess that means you don't want to hear what the *SS* people told me then, huh?"

"No," she replied. "Not now anyway. You can tell me on the way home."

"Okay. Hey, speaking of the trip home, how 'bout we drive down to St. Augustine after we leave Clayton and have lunch at the inn where we spent our honeymoon? Remember how much you loved it there, baby?"

Jess remembered it all too well and had to swallow the lump that appeared in her throat at the memory. "I know what you're trying to do, Lee, and that's not the way to solve our problems. You can't romance me out of the way I feel."

"That's not what I'm doing. I just want you to remember how it was for us when we were there. We didn't care about eating or sleeping or anything except *us*. Isn't that the way you want it to be again?"

"Yes, but not just for an afternoon every now and then when you need to score points with me. I'd rather not have it at all than have it that way."

"Don't we have to start somewhere?" he said. "Can't we start with today and work our way up to always?"

Jess knew better than to look at him, so she stared straight ahead. "I'll let you know when we leave the library." When she saw Lee looking at the cameo on her collar, she touched it and said, "Lexie gave it to me. Isn't it incredible?"

"Yeah. You had it on yesterday too, didn't you?"

She nodded. "I may not ever take it off. I told Lexie it would remind me of her spirit and amazing strength. I really do love it."

He squeezed Jess's arm. "I'll tell her you said that. I know it'll mean a lot to her to know something she did made a difference for someone."

They managed to talk about non-volatile things

until they reached Clayton, a little town on the outskirts of Jacksonville whose economy revolved around Winters College. Lee told her it was a modest-sized school, but it had an excellent baseball program that had even produced a few major league players.

"Anyone I'd know?" she asked.

He fingered his chin. "Hmm…no, I don't think Babe Ruth went there, so you wouldn't know any of them."

She scoffed. "I know more players than that. Who's that guy with the Braves you like so much? Chippy Jones?"

His laughter almost made him run off the road. "It's *Chipper*, Jess. And please don't let anyone at work hear you call him that. We'd be run out of town on a rail."

Chapter Thirteen

They found the library in Clayton and went inside to wait for Cara by the periodicals as she and Jess had agreed. Lee picked up the copy of *The Hair-Pulling Problem* Jess had brought and flipped through it while they waited.

"Man, Jess. This says there are eight million people in the U.S. alone that have this trich stuff. How come I've never heard about it before?"

She shrugged. "Most of the people who have it are ashamed to talk about it because they're afraid of ridicule. A lot of them think it's a mental deficiency they have to hide, and there's not enough information out there to change that perception."

He tucked a lock of her hair behind her ear. "Do you really think you have it, Jess? Your hair doesn't look any different than it ever did."

"That's only because I have so much hair. I'm controlling it with the things I learned from this book, but if I'd kept going at the rate I was pulling before, I'd probably have a bald spot on my crown by now."

Despite his lack of reproach, she couldn't help the awkwardness she felt at admitting how much hair she'd pulled. How did people with no support from their families ever manage to do it?

His surprise at her confession quickly dissolved into remorse. "This is my fault, isn't it? I'm the one who causes all your stress."

"No, Lee. You definitely make me want to pull out my hair sometimes, but this is different." She elbowed him with a snicker. "I know it's hard for you to believe you're not the reason for everything I do and the center of my universe, but this has nothing to do with you."

"Well, in that case it doesn't interest me at all, so let's stop talking about it." He closed the book and winked at her.

She laughed and decided to let him take her to lunch in St. Augustine before they went home. He was being so sweet and attentive, and she wanted it to last as long as possible.

"I hope nothing happened to Cara," Jess said, looking at her watch. "She should've been here by now."

"How will you know her when you see her?" Lee asked. "Do you know what she looks like?"

"I've seen her picture online, and she said she'd be wearing a purple beret."

"How will she know you?"

"I told her I'd be the redhead waiting with a blond guy talking nonstop about himself."

He narrowed his eyes at her. "Okay, then let me tell you all about my workout with Trent yesterday at the gym. I couldn't decide whether to start with curls or bench presses, so I—"

She laughed and shushed him because the librarian was giving them the evil eye.

Cara arrived a few minutes later. Jess waved to get her attention, and she hurried over to where they were sitting.

"Sorry I'm late, Jess. My uncle got called in to

work at the last minute, so I had to beg my dad to bring me."

Jess could tell the girl had been crying and got up to hug her. "It's okay, Cara. We haven't been here that long. This is my husband Lee."

Cara flushed and said, "Oh, hi." She lowered her gaze and pulled down on the beret.

Lee took one of her hands in both of his. "It's good to meet you, Cara. I can't believe how much you remind me of my little sister Lexie."

She looked up, her face brightening. "Oh, Lexie's so great. We've been writing to each other all week, and I already feel like I've known her forever. She thinks you're the best brother in the world."

Jess could have kissed Lee for knowing the perfect thing to say that would make him less intimidating to Cara. She had to settle for giving him a grateful smile as the three of them sat down at the table together, but she made a mental note to reward him later.

"Where's your father now, Cara?" Jess asked. "Do you want to introduce us?"

"Oh, *no*," she replied. "He thinks I'm paying a fine for a library book. He'd have a fit if he knew this was anything to do with my hair. He's waiting in the car, so I can't stay long."

Jess sighed and handed her the book. "Okay, sweetie. I want you to read this from cover to cover, then e-mail me when you're done. We'll go on with your treatment plan from there."

"I will, and thank you so much for doing this." Cara hugged the book to her chest briefly before putting it in her tote bag. "I promise I'll do everything it says so I can be normal like you, Jess. Your hair is so pretty."

Jess put a hand on Cara's arm. "The first thing I want you to do is believe that you're already normal. You simply have a physical condition to manage, Cara, just like someone with diabetes. This book will help you see that."

"Besides," Lee added, "you should see Jess's hair first thing in the morning. Talk about abnormal."

Jess shoved him, and the tears that had been threatening in Cara's eyes a moment earlier were gone with her laughter. Jess laughed with her and gave Lee another grateful smile. He really did have a knack for putting people at ease.

"I guess I'd better go," Cara said. She hugged Jess and paused only briefly before hugging Lee too. "Lexie and Jess are lucky to have you. And they're right about you being a hunk too."

"Hey, I didn't say that about him," Jess protested. "I said *he* thinks he's a hunk."

Lee laughed. "Give it up, baby. Your cover's blown."

They walked to the library's entrance with Cara and hung back at her request so she could go outside alone, but they watched her through the double glass doors. She ran over to a station wagon, and Jess could tell from the expression on her father's face that he started grilling her as soon as she got in.

Cara shook her head several times then appeared to be struggling with him over her tote bag. He jerked it away and took out the book Jess had given her, shaking it at her until she covered her face with her hands. When the man rolled down his window and tossed out the book, Lee was out the door before Jess could stop him.

She ran after him across the parking lot, glad he was going to confront the man but afraid of the outcome. Lee picked up the book then jerked open the driver's side door, interrupting Cara's father in the middle of yelling at her that he was tired of her craziness.

"What the hell is wrong with you, mister?" Lee thrust the book in front of the startled man's face. "You need to read every word of this to help your daughter instead of yelling at her!"

"Who are you people?" The man scowled and looked from Lee to where Jess had gone around the car to console Cara. "This is none of your business!"

"Cara and I met online," Jess said, "in a forum for people with trichotillomania—the condition we both have that makes us pull out our hair. That book was written by a doctor who's treated thousands of people like us, and Cara needs it. Especially since she has a father who calls her crazy!"

The man looked at Lee again. "And who are you? The hair club's bouncer?"

Lee smiled unpleasantly. "If I need to be. I don't know much about any of this stuff myself, but if my wife says your daughter needs this book, then you can bet the farm on it, buddy. They don't come any smarter than Jess."

Cara turned pleading eyes to her father. "Please let me keep the book, Daddy. I'm sorry I didn't tell you the truth about why I wanted to come here today, but I knew you wouldn't bring me if I told you."

He took the book from Lee and read the cover. "You say this doctor has cured people of this craziness before?"

Jess forced herself to answer him civilly. "It's not a disease that can be cured, but it's also not craziness or a mental illness. There are drugs that can help with anxiety and stress, but the treatment methods in this book have helped thousands of people stop pulling their hair without using any drugs at all. I know because I'm one of them."

"You mean it's just a matter of self-control, and she could've stopped a long time ago if she really wanted to?" He tossed the book on the seat and looked disgusted. "Just like I figured."

"No, that's *not* all there is to it. This is no different from a diet and exercise plan prescribed by a doctor to manage a physical illness. I'm sure you wouldn't be so callous and insensitive about it if Cara were diabetic."

"Look, lady." He pointed a finger at Jess. "Don't try to tell me I don't care about my daughter. I've already wasted all kinds of money sending her to doctors, and it didn't do a damn bit of good. Just look at her!" He snatched the beret from Cara's head and revealed huge bald patches at her crown and behind her ears.

Cara cried out and tried to cover her head with her hands as Jess put her arms around the poor girl, but before she could say anything to Cara's father about what he'd done, Lee had already yanked the man out of the car by his shirt.

"Lee, don't hit him!" Jess said. "I don't blame you for wanting to, but please don't!"

"Listen to your wife, mister," Cara's father said in a voice shaky with fear.

Lee's face was thrust into the cowering man's, but he pulled him closer still until their noses were almost touching. "I ought to beat the living hell out of you for doing that to her. My wife is the *only* reason I'm not gonna do it, so you're the one who'd better listen to her. You got that?"

"Okay, sure," the man said. "No problem."

Lee let him go and snatched the beret from his hand to give it back to Jess. "And don't try to play the part of the concerned father if you can do something like that to your own daughter." He gestured at Cara sobbing in Jess's arms. "I know what a father's supposed to be like because I had a great one. You don't even deserve to claim the title."

The man had the decency to look ashamed as he got back into the car, hastily closing the door and locking it.

"Look, you don't know what it's like to watch your only child doing something like this to herself. She won't take the drugs the doctors gave her because she claims they keep her from being able to 'create.' What the hell is that supposed to mean?"

"If you paid attention to her," Jess said, "you might know the answer to that." Since he obviously didn't know about Cara's poetry or the animé artwork she did, Jess didn't think she'd want her to say anything about them. "It's bad enough that she can't rely on her doctors to help her. She should at least be able to count on her family for support."

"What am I supposed to do? She doesn't listen to me!"

"Well, for starters," Jess said, "you can go home and read that book yourself."

"And what happens if this doesn't work either? She got worse every time the doctors and the drugs didn't help. She hides in that room of hers all the time and talks about dying. You think that's what I want for my daughter?" His voice broke and he hung his head.

Cara withdrew slowly from Jess's arms and put the beret back on her head, then she turned to look at her father. "Daddy, are you…crying?"

He shook his head without lifting it and wiped his eyes with the back of his hand. "No, of course not. Don't be ridiculous."

Jess couldn't help feeling for the man even though she'd wanted to punch him herself only moments before. "Sir, I don't blame you for being afraid of more disappointment, but I know the treatment method in this book works because I use it myself. I'll help Cara every step of the way, but she needs your support more than anything."

He looked up and didn't try to hide the tears in his eyes. "I just want her to be the happy kid she used to be before all this started. I want my little girl back."

Cara reached for his hand. "I promise I'll work hard and do what the book says, Daddy. I know I can do it if you just let me try."

He picked up the book and studied it a few seconds before he handed it to her. "How 'bout we read it together when we get home? You, me, and your mama."

Chapter Fourteen

Jess managed to keep from crying until Cara and her father were gone and she was alone with Lee in his car.

"I'm sorry for blubbering like this," she said, accepting his handkerchief. "I'm just so glad she's finally getting some support from her parents."

"And she has you to thank for it, Jess. The way you stood up to that guy was great." He looked a little sheepish. "A lot smarter than beating the hell out of him."

"I don't blame you for that, Lee. Thank you for defending her, and for what you said to him about me."

He took the handkerchief from her and wiped her cheek. "You know I've always thought you were the smartest cookie in the basket."

She gave him a tearful smile. "Cookies usually go in jars, but thanks for saying that."

"Jars, baskets, whatever." He kissed her on the end of her nose. "You're amazing no matter what the container."

Her earlier surge of affection for him returned. "Take me to St. Augustine, Lee."

He looked surprised for a moment, then a smile spread across his face. "Your wish is my command, Mrs. Cassady."

A little before noon, they arrived at the Lion's Gate

Inn, the quaint bed and breakfast in the historical district of America's oldest city where they'd stayed on their honeymoon. Jess was transported back to the week they'd spent taking horse-drawn carriage rides, browsing the art galleries and antique shops on the sun-dappled streets, and watching the sunset from their balcony while wrapped in each other's arms in the drowsy afterglow of lovemaking. She hadn't been able to imagine ever being happier than she'd been that week, and she thought maybe that was part of their problem. No marriage could sustain that kind of perfection for long.

When they entered the Lion's Den restaurant, Lee told the hostess he had reservations for the private dining area on the west verandah overlooking the bay. Jess arched an eyebrow at him as they followed the hostess to their table.

"Reservations, Lee? Sure of yourself as usual."

He tucked her hand in his arm. "Optimistic, my love. You know what they say about the power of positive thinking."

A waiter appeared after they were seated and told them the chef had been notified of their arrival and had begun preparation of the food Lee had ordered in advance. He returned a few moments later with a bottle of champagne and two fluted glasses.

"I should be mad at you for assuming so much," Jess said, "but since you've been so nice today and this is too wonderful to resist, I'll let you off the hook."

Lee touched his glass to hers. "Gracious as well as smart and beautiful. I'm a lucky man indeed."

She took a sip of champagne, then she took two more to boost the mellowness of her mood. "Tell me about the job with *Sports Spotlight*. What did they say?"

He set down his glass and leaned forward. "Well, they didn't bite on the two-for-one deal I pitched, but since you said you didn't want to work for them anyway, I didn't sweat that. Plus they told me they liked the hummus I demonstrated by asking."

She bit her lip to keep from laughing. "I'm sure it was your *hubris* they liked, Lee, but go on."

"Hubris, right. So they told me they're hiring correspondents to cover the baseball teams that usually make it to the pennant races and that writers who live near one of the franchises would have an advantage since they wouldn't need to relocate." He paused and took her hand. "They're considering me to cover the Braves for them."

Jess struggled to process exactly what the job would entail. "As a permanent position or just this year?"

"For as long as the Braves stay consistently in the running, and that's not likely to change any time soon. I could even keep working for the paper when it wasn't baseball season. And I know Thad would always let me come back full time if I needed to."

Jess thought about it and nodded. "It does sound perfect for you."

Relief washed over his face. "I'm glad you feel that way, baby. I really think this is a job we can both be happy about. I'm trying to do whatever you want me to do so I can come back home."

"I don't want you doing things just to pacify me, Lee. I want us to have the same priorities."

"We do when it counts, Jess. You're my top

priority and I'm yours. Isn't that what matters?" He seemed sincere, and his eyes searched her face with hope that she didn't want to dash.

"Of course it matters, Lee, but you have to prove it to me with more than just words."

"Don't you believe me?" he said. "You know I wouldn't lie to you."

She shook her head. "I don't know what I believe. I'm still trying to sort out my feelings about a lot of things and deal with some issues of my own."

"Like what? Just tell me and I'll take care of it for you."

"It doesn't work that way. I need to handle things myself."

"You might be surprised about that." He leaned back with a smug little smile that she didn't like at all. "I might even have taken care of some of them for you already."

"What are you talking about?" she said. "What have you done?"

He waved away her question as the waiter arrived with a platter of crab claws—more of Lee's advance planning. After sampling one, Jess discovered how hungry she was and let their conversation rest as she polished off more than half the platter while Lee watched her in amusement.

"See, I pay attention sometimes," he said. "I ordered these because I know you can eat your weight in them." He took one of the few remaining claws and dipped it in cocktail sauce.

"You're observant if not tactful. So nice of you to point out my gluttony."

He laughed. "Nah, you don't weigh enough for it to

qualify as gluttony."

"Nice recovery." She finished the last one on her plate. "Thank you, Lee. For this and everything else."

"Save all your gratitude for when we get home." He leaned across and put his hand over hers. "You can thank me then."

The look in his eyes conveyed exactly what he had in mind, and her body reacted the same way it had the first time he'd asked her to spend the night with him when they were in college. And she doubted she could resist him this time any more than she had then. If she had any intention of remaining objective where he was concerned, she knew she shouldn't even let him come in the house when they got back, but she wasn't sure she could be that strong.

The food was delicious, the view was stunning, and Lee couldn't have been more attentive. When they left the restaurant, Jess practically floated to the car on his arm, and she didn't miss the way he pointedly ignored the admiring looks he got from the other female patrons. He was definitely going all out to charm her, and it was definitely working.

He opened the car door for her but stopped her before she could get in. "Once we get everything worked out between us, I want to bring you back here for a second honeymoon. We'll make it even better than the first one and start all over. Okay, Jess?"

With considerable difficulty, she managed to resist sending him back inside to see if they had a room available for the afternoon.

"That would be wonderful if things work out, Lee."

His smile faded. "Why are you still saying *if*? How much more proof do you need that I love you?"

"That's never been the problem. But this isn't the place to talk about it."

"Fine. The hell with talking." He put his arms around her and tried to kiss her, but she put her hands on his chest and turned her face away.

"Don't, Lee. Let's just go."

When she saw the injured look on his face, she almost regretted stopping him, and his expression didn't change as he walked around the car to the driver's side. They both got in, but he made no move to start the engine, staring instead at his hands on the steering wheel for a few seconds before turning to look at her with a frustrated sigh.

"I give up, Jess. I've done everything I can think of to get you to take me back, and you're still pushing me away. You say you believe I love you but it's not enough. Well, I don't have a clue what else you want from me. If today didn't convince you that we belong together, then I guess we might as well call it quits."

His sudden mood change surprised her. "I'm sorry you feel that way, Lee. I thought we were making good progress today."

"You won't even let me kiss you. You call that progress?"

"I meant we were doing a better job of talking and listening to each other. Kissing won't solve anything."

"Damn it, Jess! Do you love me or not?"

"What does that have to do with anything?" She realized how stupid it sounded as soon as it was out of her mouth. Lee's incredulous expression told her he had the same opinion.

"It's the *only* thing that matters," he said. "If you love me, then stop torturing me like this and let me come home."

She hated seeing his misery, especially since she did love him. She also felt like the biggest hypocrite in the world because she could admit it to herself and to Deb, but not to him. Feeling her resolve about to crumble, she tried to stall.

"You can come inside when we get back home, Lee. We'll talk about everything there."

"No." He took her by the shoulders and pulled her to him. "If you can't tell me you love me right now, then I'm done talking."

"Lee—"

He pulled her closer until their lips were almost touching. "Say you love me or say you don't. No more games, Jess."

She stared at him a moment before squeezing her eyes shut. No matter how hard she'd tried to convince them both that she could live without him, the truth was she'd been hopelessly in love with him since the first time he'd kissed her. She might not ever get him to understand everything she'd been trying to tell him, but she was tired of pretending she wanted to be anywhere but his arms. She opened her eyes and looked into his.

"Of course I love you, you stupid jerk. I've always loved you too much for my own good."

She didn't resist when he kissed her this time.

In fact, she forgot where they were and anything that had happened prior to the instant his lips touched hers and everything that was important became clear again.

She stopped fighting and gave herself over to the strongest force she'd ever had in her life—her love for this man who made her both utterly miserable and blissfully happy. The man who owned her heart.

"My Jess," he murmured against her neck. "I knew you still loved me."

"Let's go home, Lee."

Chapter Fifteen

They barely spoke during the high-speed drive back to Georgia, as if they were both afraid of sabotaging their reconciliation with words. Jess didn't let herself think about anything except how it had felt to be back in the arms of the man who had uncovered the passionate stores inside her and shown her how to tap into them with abandon—the only part of her life where she'd never been bound by inhibitions.

But the quiet restraint lasted only until they were inside the house, because as soon as the front door closed behind them, Lee pinned her against it with his body and kissed her with an unrelenting insistence she'd never felt from him before. He usually gave her free rein and let her be the aggressor, but they'd been apart too long for him to concede control to her this time. She felt both their hearts beating in a percussive accompaniment to the frenzied dance of Lee's hands as they unbuttoned her blouse and removed her bra, and he couldn't go fast enough to suit her. She willed his fingers to work faster, her veins struggling to contain the blood that raced through them on its way to all the places he sought to uncover. But as soon as his hands touched her bare skin, she had to free her mouth from his to catch her breath.

"Lee, the bedroom…"

"No, I want you right here." His lips traveled down

her throat as her slacks fell from her hips. "I want you in every room of *our* house, on every piece of furniture and every floor. We'll get to the bed later."

She smiled and pushed up his shirt to run her hands over the hard contours of his chest, his barely contained need for her making his body practically vibrate beneath her fingers. She had always relished the feel of his muscles. The thought of the raw strength within them was an incredible turn-on for her, and she loved knowing that such a powerful man belonged completely to her and would so willingly let himself end up helpless in her arms.

He backed away long enough to shed his own clothes, and she feared for a moment that she would faint from the blood rush that hit her at the sight of his naked body. He was truly the most beautiful man she'd ever seen. But just as her knees threatened to give way on her, she found herself once again pinned between the door and her husband's unyielding body, his mouth reclaiming hers with a force that left no possibility of protest had she even considered it.

His hands were doing magical things to her breasts, and long before she was ready to escape their exquisite captivity, they slid down her body to wrap her legs around him. He lifted her hips and held them poised above his, then he looked into her eyes with his breath coming in rapid puffs against her face.

"You're mine, Jess. Don't ever forget that again. You've been mine since the first time I kissed you, and I haven't wanted anybody but you since that moment. We love each other, and *this* is all that matters."

She cried out as he simultaneously lowered her hips and pressed upward with his, their bodies reuniting as though they'd never been apart. And despite the familiar temporary insanity that overtook her while he moved them both in a rhythm that was much too divine to sustain for long, and even as she approached the point where all she could do was clutch him and murmur his name over and over, she couldn't help thinking how incredibly stupid she had been to think she could ever give him up.

****

She was still awake at two the next morning, after they'd finally made it to the bed. She'd always loved the euphoric time after lovemaking, lying in the circle of Lee's arms with her ear against his chest as she listened to the sweet lullaby of his heartbeat and his breathing. She matched her own breaths to his the way she always did and snuggled a little closer to him.

"Don't go, Jess." His arms tightened around her. "Stay here next to me."

"I'm not going anywhere, Lee. Go back to sleep." She ran her hands over his chest until his breathing became even again. He'd definitely earned his rest over the past few hours, but although she was exhausted as well, she wanted to stay awake a little longer and savor the wonder of having him back.

They had even managed to talk some in the intervals between lovemaking. Funny how their problems seemed so much smaller when discussed in the afterglow of ecstasy. He'd promised to be more sensitive to her feelings, and she'd promised to give him credit for effort as long as she believed it was genuine. She knew him too well not to expect any slipups, but she couldn't go on denying that she loved him despite his faults. As long as the good times outnumbered the bad, she could forgive him for his mistakes.

As she drifted off to sleep, she smiled at the memory of one particularly good time they'd had a little earlier, and Lee woke her at dawn for an encore.

****

Jess made waffles for breakfast, and they ate them while they worked the Sunday crossword puzzle the way they'd always done it together: Jess provided the answers and Lee wrote them down. He wanted her to go with him to retrieve his things from Trent's, but after a joint shower and the resulting delays it caused, most of the day was gone before they knew it. She sent him to Trent's with the promise of steak for dinner when he returned. He called while she was making the salad.

"I'm all packed and ready to leave, baby. Put the food in the oven to keep it warm and take off all your clothes."

"Filet mignon is too expensive to turn into shoe leather, Lee. You'll have to make it an after-dinner performance."

"I'd pick you over food any day," he said. "We can always split a bowl of Cheerios later. What do you say?"

"I'm flattered, but I'm feeling rather carnivorous after cooking these steaks. I don't want to waste them."

"Well, okay," he said morosely. "I'll force myself to eat for your sake. See you in a few."

She hung up and the phone rang again almost immediately.

"Can we at least eat in the buff?" he asked.

She laughed. "No, stupid. Hurry up and come home. I'm starving." When the phone rang again, she picked it up and said, "Lee, I'm going to change my mind about taking you back if you don't hurry up and get here."

Silence. Then Noah's voice: "I guess this means our date is off."

Jess dropped the salad tongs she was holding. "Oh, Noah, I thought you were—oh, you don't need me to tell you that. I'm sorry, I…" She tried in vain to think of something appropriate to say.

"It's okay, Jess. You don't owe me an explanation. To tell the truth, I'm not really surprised. He said he'd have you back before the end of the month, so I guess he was right."

"When did he say that?" A seed of worry sprouted into a frown on Jess's face. "Where did you see him?"

"Never mind. It's not important now."

"It's important to me, Noah. When did you talk to Lee?"

He sighed. "After the lecture the other night. He pulled up right after you drove away and said he wanted to talk to me man-to-man."

Jess sat at the table with one hand on her forehead. "Did he hurt you?"

"No, he was actually a lot more reasonable than the first time we met. He didn't offer to break or smash any body parts. He just told me how stupid I was to think I could compete with him for you. As I recall, he used some kind of analogy that started out about baseball and ended with telling me he'd be parking in his own garage again before the month was over."

Jess felt her color rise along with her temper. "Yes, he has an unsurpassed talent for mixing metaphors. I'm sorry you had to listen to his rantings, Noah."

"I take it from the way you answered the phone that you've decided to forgive his past transgressions."

She was glad she didn't have to see the look on his face. "I thought we'd worked through all our problems, but now I'm not so sure. At least he didn't threaten you this time."

"Well, I can't say I'm happy for you, but I do wish you the best. And if things don't work out for some reason, please give me a call."

"I will, Noah. Thank you for being so understanding."

She hung up and found her appetite had disappeared with the prospect of confronting Lee about all of it when he got home. They'd been so happy for the past twenty-four hours that she hated for it to end, but she couldn't just ignore what he'd done. Since he'd so conveniently forgotten to mention his clandestine meeting with Noah, she had to wonder what else he was keeping from her.

She finished the salad and put it in the refrigerator, then she went to wait for Lee in the bedroom, where the positive vibes were the strongest and ended up dozing off. She woke to find Lee kissing her neck.

"Well, you didn't lose the clothes," he said, "but at least you're in the right room." When she didn't smile, he said, "What's wrong, baby?"

"I know about your conversation with Noah after the lecture the other night. What were you doing there, and when were you planning to tell me about it?"

"He came over here?" The muscles in his jaw twitched noticeably.

"No, he called. Answer my question, Lee."

He rolled onto his back with a sigh. "What's the

big deal, Jess? I didn't hit him or anything."

"I know that. If you had, I wouldn't have let you back in the house."

He gave her a dark look. "Speaking of being more sensitive to each other's feelings, how the hell do you think it makes me feel when you take up for some guy who's just trying to get in your pants?"

"He is *not*." She shoved him. "That was crude and nothing but a weak attempt at diverting attention from what you did."

"I didn't do anything except talk to him. A blind man could see he's got the hots for you, but he even admitted it. You think I was just gonna stand by and let him get his hands on you?"

She narrowed her eyes. "Is that why you've been trying so hard with me lately? Just to keep some other guy from parking in your garage?"

"I see he blabbed to you about everything I said. I should've kicked his ass like I wanted to do in the first place, even though it would've been like squashing a bug."

She stood up and hit him with one of the throw pillows from the bed. "You know I hate it when you act like a barbarian. It really shows how well you know me."

"Actually it does, Mrs. Cassady." He took the pillow from her and propped his head with it. "No matter how much you pretend to be outraged and scandalized, I know how much it lights your fire whenever I threaten anybody who messes with you."

Her anger was stoked by her inability to deny it. Although it went completely against the few feminist sensibilities she could claim, Lee's machismo had always been a big part of his attraction for her. Of all the things for him to be perceptive about, she couldn't believe he'd picked up on something so embarrassing that she didn't even want to own up to it to herself. And she definitely wasn't going to admit it to him now.

"You're crazy, Lee. And you still haven't answered my question. What were you doing at the lecture in the first place? Stalking me?"

He shrugged. "I followed you because I figured he'd be there. I was right, wasn't I?"

She put her hands on her hips. "I should've known all this attention you've been paying me was just an act so you could defeat Noah in some kind of macho competition going on inside your immature little brain."

"Then I must be one helluva good actor for you to let me make love to you so many times since we got home yesterday." He got up and pulled her against him with an arm around her waist. "Guess we know who won the contest, huh?"

She looked into his eyes with all the scorn she could manage. "Right, Lee. You win the prize for best performance by a lying husband."

"I haven't lied to you about anything. I love you and meant every word I've said."

"But what else *haven't* you said? That's what worries me."

His gaze flitted away for a split second before he answered.

"Nothing. Now can we please go eat the steaks you didn't want to ruin?"

She searched his face for more signs of deception. When he kissed her suddenly, as if to escape any further scrutiny, it only reinforced her suspicions. But she was still too much in the throes of their reignited passion not to respond to his kiss, and she wanted desperately to believe him so they could get back to the happiness they'd found again at last.

They loved each other—hadn't he made her see that was all that really mattered? Her heart and her body said yes, but the mocking voice in her head calling her a fool and telling her she was just some kind of macho trophy made her push him away.

"Stop it, Lee. I won't let you seduce me into stupidity again. You can eat if you want to. I seem to have lost my appetite."

He left the room with an exasperated sigh. Jess lay on the bed listening to him banging things around in the kitchen, bitterly thinking how different their future seemed now compared to an hour earlier when he'd left for Trent's. She wished she could pretend she hadn't seen Lee's guilty reaction to her question and didn't feel certain he was hiding something else from her. Maybe their only chance for happiness was if she let him blind her with the bliss she found in his arms and didn't worry about anything else.

She decided to take a bath and try to dissolve her worries in a mountain of Moonlight Path-scented bubbles, part of the pampering she'd grown so fond of indulging in while she'd been an independent woman. Soaking in the hot water did help ease her tension, but when the water became tepid she got out to get ready for bed. Lee came into the bedroom while she was rubbing lotion on her legs.

"I cleaned up and put the food away," he said. "You're still not gonna eat anything?"

She shook her head. "I'm not hungry."

He walked tentatively around the bed and sat down. "Want me to rub some of that on your feet for you, baby?" He ran a finger across the top of her toes and looked at her with scolded puppy dog eyes. "Gotta keep these model feet soft and subtle, you know."

"Soft and *supple*, Lee." She couldn't help snickering. "And you know I can't resist a foot rub. Even from a sneaky, immature barbarian like you."

He grinned and took the bottle of lotion from her. "Hey, I know a game we can play when I'm done. I'll be Conan, and you can be the queen who tries to civilize me."

She propped one foot on his thigh. "No, I'll be Jess on vacation, and you can be my favorite cabana boy."

He tossed the lotion bottle aside and covered her body with his. "Your *only* cabana boy, Mrs. Cassady. Eager to please and desperate for a tip."

"Then you'd better not forget the foot rub afterward," she said before letting him kiss her.

She put her arms around his neck and closed her eyes, determined to forget everything except how much she loved him and the way he made her feel. Yes, she'd only think about times like this and wouldn't worry about anything else. He'd probably kept his conversation with Noah a secret because he was embarrassed for her to know how jealous he was, so there was really no reason for her to think he was hiding anything else.

She kept telling herself that and almost convinced herself to believe it, until much later when he was drifting off to sleep. She lay with her head on his chest, listening to his heartbeat.

"Lee, promise you won't keep anything else from

me, okay?"

"Um-hmm," he murmured. "Sleep now, baby. Talk later."

It wasn't his answer that bothered her, even though it was damned evasive. What bothered her was the way she'd heard his heartbeat speed up when she'd asked him. That kept her awake for a long time.

Chapter Sixteen

The next few days were filled with tense civility. Jess tried to give Lee the benefit of the doubt while she waited for him to drop a bomb on her about what else he'd done behind her back. And Lee continued acting as if he had no idea why she would even suspect him of anything.

If she'd ever questioned how much stress affected her ability to control her hair pulling, she certainly believed it now. Still, she thought she was doing a good job of hiding her hyper-stressed state until Deb cornered her in the ladies' room at work on Wednesday.

"Okay, spill it, girlfriend." Deb folded her arms and frowned at Jess in the room-length mirror. "Why do I get the feeling you're having second thoughts about letting the prodigal husband return to the domicile?"

"I don't have any idea what you're talking about." Jess concentrated on washing her hands and avoided Deb's accusing gaze. "I told you Lee and I got everything worked out. Didn't you say you thought the correspondent job was a good compromise?"

"Yeah, so why do you look like you're next in line for a root canal every time he's in the same room with you?"

Jess tried to look nonchalant. "He just keeps me off kilter. I forgot it wasn't easy working with someone I sleep with."

Deb grimaced. "Yeah, in his case I can see how that would make you look perpetually nauseated."

Jess managed to escape any further interrogation, but the exchange told her that if Deb had noticed her tension around Lee, he had to have noticed it himself. His failure to mention it only served to make Jess more suspicious that he was hiding something.

That night while they ate dinner, she decided she couldn't take it any longer. "Lee, I know there's something you're not telling me. I promise to keep an open mind if you come clean."

"I don't know what you mean, Jess. Why do you think I'm hiding something?" His expression was a little too bewildered to be believable.

"You're only making things worse by putting it off, so just tell me." She tried to look receptive even though she was ready to throttle him.

He stared at the jambalaya on his plate, then he gave her a smile that looked deliberately disarming. "You know me too well, don't you, baby? There is one little thing I need to tell you about the job offer from *Sports Spotlight*."

The initial relief she felt at knowing it had nothing to do with Noah didn't last long. "I knew there was something. What is it?"

"It's nothing really. Just a little trip I have to make if they hire me."

She arched one eyebrow. "A little trip to where?"

"To the *SS* offices in New York."

"For how long?"

He reached across the table and took her hand. "Two weeks."

"Why?"

"For training on their style manual. They said it's required for all their writers."

She wasn't happy about it by any means, but it wasn't nearly as bad as the things she'd been imagining. She looked at him with a resigned sigh.

"Well, I think that's a ridiculous amount of time for training, but I guess you wouldn't have a choice if it's required." When he didn't release her hand, she realized there was more. "What else, Lee?"

He kept his gaze on their hands. "There's also some travel involved in the job itself."

"How much?"

"I'd have to follow the Braves whenever they're on the road."

"How many road games do they play?"

He swallowed visibly. "Eighty-one."

"God, Lee. You might as well move out again."

"No, it won't be that bad. I'll be home in between trips, and they said you can go with me to some of the games. I know we can make it work, baby."

Something about the way he'd phrased it made her suddenly feel queasy.

"You've already taken the job, haven't you? You'd already taken it before you ever told me about it!"

His hesitation was all the reply she needed. She snatched her hand from his and stood up.

"You're unbelievable, Lee."

"Jess, wait." He followed her to the bedroom and stopped her before she could shut the door. "I swear I was planning to tell you when I got back from Trent's Sunday night, but when I found out you were already pissed at me for telling your wimpy boyfriend to back off, I knew you'd blow a gasket over this. I was just waiting for the right time to tell you."

"That's not even the point, Lee. You haven't paid a bit of attention to anything I told you while we were separated or you wouldn't have taken a job like this without at least talking to me about it first." She pushed him aside and sat on the bed. "You promised things would be different and we would make decisions like this together, but you didn't even care enough about what I thought to ask me before you took the job."

He sat beside her on the bed. "No, that's not how it was. When they made me the offer, you were still talking about divorcing me. I didn't know if you'd ever let me come home."

"And you thought excluding me from this decision was the way to prove how important I am to you?"

"No, but they wanted an answer quick, and I'd already missed out on one job with them because of—" He winced. "I didn't mean it that way, Jess."

"Oh, I know you didn't mean to say it. It's always an accident when you tell me the truth."

He hung his head. "Don't make me leave again, Jess."

"I don't care what you do. Just leave me alone."

He looked up, his surprise evident. "You're letting me stay?"

"Sure, Lee. Why waste my time with a lawyer when I can just wait for you to start your new job? You'll be gone all the time and I can do whatever I want, plus I'll get to spend all your money. This is a much better solution than a divorce, don't you think?" She stood up to go into the bathroom and snatched away her hand when he tried to take it. "Don't touch me. Just because I'm not kicking you out doesn't mean

I'm not furious with you. I may be too stupid to stop loving you no matter how many times you disappoint me, but I'm sure as hell not letting you use me."

"Jess, I know you're mad right now, but this job won't be as bad as you think. We can—"

She slammed the bathroom door to cut him off and turned on the water in the tub full blast, then she knelt beside it and rested her head on the cold porcelain. Why was she so stupid? She should've known he'd go back to his selfishness as soon as he was sure he had her back in his grips. And she only rated his full attention as long as it didn't conflict with his precious career plans.

****

Lee gave up quickly the next morning when his attempts at reconciliation were met with stony silence. They took separate cars to work, so Jess didn't see him again until right before lunch when she went to ask Thad a question about an article she was working on and almost collided with Lee as he came out of Thad's office.

"Oh—hi, Jess," Thad said. "Lee and I were just talking about his new career venture. Are you as proud of our boy as I am?" He slapped Lee on the back and grinned.

"I really can't answer that right now," she said. "I think I'm still in shock."

Lee cleared his throat. "Um, I'd better get back to work. Thanks again, Thad."

"Hold on a second." Thad put an arm across Jess's shoulders. "I want to hear what Jess thinks about her husband jet-setting off for a weekend at the Waldorf Astoria. You think he'll come back to us after rubbing shoulders with the *SS* brass this weekend?"

Lee looked as though he'd eaten some expired pork.

"Your guess is as good as mine," Jess said. "I'm never quite sure what to expect from him."

Lee excused himself and managed to get away, but he was waiting for Jess around the corner when she left Thad's office a few minutes later. She tried to impale him with a look and walk past him, but he grabbed her arm and stopped her.

"I swear I didn't know anything about this trip until Cassandra Wilhelm called me after I got to work this morning. I was gonna tell you as soon as we got home tonight."

"Sure, I understand, Lee. It's a lot more important to go brag to your boss about something like this before you talk to your wife. I mean, it's not like we work down the hall from each other and there was any chance I'd get blindsided by hearing about it secondhand, right?" She pulled her arm from his grasp and walked away.

"Okay, I screwed up again and I'm sorry, Jess. Go to lunch with me so we can talk about it."

She ducked into the ladies' room to get away from him. Leaning against the door inside one of the stalls, she summoned every breathing and relaxation technique she knew in an effort to keep herself from hyperventilating. When she could breathe somewhat normally again, she slipped into the copyediting office to retrieve her purse and left before Deb could get off the phone and grill her.

She had no desire to eat anything, so she drove to a little park she went to on her lunch hour sometimes when she wanted to read uninterrupted. She parked in a shady spot in one of the far corners where she could be miserable in private. Lee had played her deftly, that was for sure. He must've known that once he seduced her into letting him come back home, he could stop pretending to care about what she wanted and go back to treating her like an afterthought.

But what really made her furious with herself was knowing that she wouldn't kick him out again, no matter how mad she was right now. Hadn't she decided when she'd let him come home that she could take the bad along with the good? And the truth was that if it weren't for the times like their honeymoon and the lunch date in St. Augustine when he'd been so wonderful, she wouldn't be nearly as disappointed the rest of the time when he was so much less than perfect.

It was almost as if he were two different men—one she wanted to be with more than anyone in the world, and one she could barely stand to be around. Maybe this job would be the answer to their problems after all. Maybe if he was gone all the time, he'd always be the Lee she loved when he was home.

She had a killer headache because of the scant two hours of sleep she'd had the night before, so she took the rest of the day off and went home to lie down. When she woke several hours later, she was greeted by the smell of bacon and eggs—the only things Lee knew how to cook. She put the pillow over her head and tried to go back to sleep, but she heard him come in the room a few minutes later and sit on the bed beside her.

"Jess, baby, I fixed supper." He moved the pillow and pushed the hair away from her face. "You hungry?"

Before she could tell him no, her stomach

reminded her that she'd skipped lunch. "I guess I could eat a little." She rolled away from him and sat up on the other side of the bed.

She knew he was only being solicitous so she would forgive him, but she decided to take advantage of his groveling and let him wait on her before she told him she wasn't mad anymore. While they ate, she listened in detached silence to his account of the phone call he'd received that morning summoning him to New York for a special meeting of all the new correspondents.

"I asked them if you could come with me, but they said no. I guess because they're footing the bill for all the expenses. At least it's not costing us anything, right?"

She shrugged. "I couldn't have missed work to go anyway. I'm working with Fred right now on his domestic abuse series."

"Oh, right. I forgot about that. Fred's lucky to be working with the best."

Yep, he was laying it on thick for sure.

"When do you have to leave?"

"My flight leaves at seven tonight."

"Nice of them to give you so much notice. Rather presumptuous if you ask me, which of course you didn't. Doesn't really bode well for the future, does it?"

He sighed. "I don't want to fight with you about it before I leave, Jess. Can't we just try to make the best of things?"

"Sure, Lee. I don't want to fight either." She stood and began clearing the table. "I'll clean up so you can go pack."

"Okay, baby. I'll hurry so we can be together

awhile before I have to leave." He gave her a look that made it clear what he had in mind.

She scoffed as she walked to the sink. "Nice try, but I don't have time. I'm going to the last installment of my lecture series tonight."

"Like hell you are!"

She turned around to look at him. "What's wrong with you?"

"You know damn well what's wrong with me. You're crazy if you think I'm letting you go cry on your boyfriend's shoulder about your lousy husband who ran off to New York without you."

"Noah won't be there tonight."

"Yeah, right. Just like he wasn't there waiting for you the last time you went."

She turned around and began rinsing the dishes again. "Well, that was before I fell for your award-winning performance and let you come back home. He knows you're living here again."

"Did you tell him not to call you or try to see you again?"

"No, but don't worry, Lee. I'm sure he'll avoid me like the plague thanks to you."

"He will if he knows what's good for him." He came over and put his arms around her waist from behind and kissed her neck. "You don't need to go to any stupid lecture anyway. Stay here so I can tell you goodbye properly."

She turned and looked up into his eyes. "Stay here with me and you won't need to tell me goodbye."

He smiled and tweaked her chin. "Wish I could, baby, but duty calls."

"Yeah, and we both know who gets priority,

right?" She turned back to the sink. "Well, I wish I could stay here and see you off, but I have things to do as well."

"I said you're not going, Jess. I wasn't kidding."

She looked at him again with her hands on her hips. "Lee, do you honestly think you can tell me what to do when you're about to run off to New York? And I don't need your permission for anything I do anyway."

"You do when it involves seeing some guy who'd just love the chance to badmouth me some more. He even tried to tell me I don't deserve you, Jess. I don't want him anywhere around you, and especially not while I'm out of town."

"Then maybe you shouldn't have taken a job that requires so much travel, huh?"

His eyes darkened and he walked over to pick up the phone. "Why don't we call him up and see what his plans are for tonight? He might want to change them after talking to me."

"I'll do no such thing, Lee. I told you I'm sure he won't be at the lecture, but it wouldn't bother me if he was. If you're allowed to do whatever you want without even discussing it with me, then I'm allowed to have friends you don't approve of."

He slammed down the phone. "Damn it, Jess! There's no comparison between the two and you know it. I said you're not going to that lecture, and that's final!"

"Don't you *dare* try to order me around, Lee Cassady. I'll do whatever I want!"

He bellowed an expletive and knocked over a chair on his way out of the kitchen. Jess had never seen him so angry before and was more than a little daunted by it, but she couldn't deny the sadistic pleasure she felt at knowing that at least he wouldn't enjoy his glamorous weekend in New York City quite as much now. And she'd be damned if she'd let him play the dictator with her. Who did he think he was? Her mother?

She took her time cleaning up, so he was just coming out of the bedroom with his suitcase when she left the kitchen. They looked at each other a moment before either of them spoke.

"I'll call you when I get checked in at the hotel," he said finally. "Will you be here?"

"I should be home from the lecture by nine."

Renewed anger darkened his features. "You know what? On second thought just forget it. Stay out all damn night if you want to."

He slammed the door behind him when he left. Jess stared at it until she heard him drive away, wondering if her defiance was worth adding to the turmoil already between them. She sighed as she retrieved Ming from her hiding place behind the loveseat and carried her to the bedroom.

"Your enemy's gone for a while, girl. Have you forgiven me yet for taking him back?"

Ming only looked up at her with feline disdain.

"Well, at least someone will have a good weekend."

An hour later, when Jess pulled into the parking lot at the junior college, she was surprised to see Noah coming out of the history building. He waved when he saw her but kept walking toward his car. She pulled into a parking space and debated briefly with herself about whether or not she should speak to him, and it didn't take long for her to decide that she wasn't willing to give up Noah's friendship just because Lee had suddenly decided to become a jealous tyrant. And she also wasn't willing to give up the independence she'd gained while she and Lee had been separated.

She got out and hurried over to Noah's car.

Chapter Seventeen

"I was hoping you'd be here tonight, Noah. It's so good to see you again."

"I had to drop off some papers for Professor Avery and was trying to make myself scarce before you arrived." His smile and the look in his eyes told her he was glad he hadn't succeeded. "I didn't want to cause you any more problems."

She put a hand on his arm. "You're not the problem, Noah. And I don't need anyone to sign off on my list of friends. I'm a big girl and I can take care of myself."

He cast a cautious glance around the parking lot. "I'm not sure your...belligerent spouse would agree with that."

"Well, that's just too bad. Besides, he's on his way to New York for a schmooze session with his new employers at *Sports Spotlight*."

Noah's eyebrows went up. "Trouble on the domestic front?"

She shrugged. "A battle of wills you might say. Look, Noah. I'd much rather listen to you than this lecture. Why don't we go get some coffee so we can talk?"

He smiled. "You won't catch me ever turning down a chance to spend time with you, Jess. Let's go."

They took his car and rode together to the Java

Joint. Once they were seated with their monster mugs in front of them, Jess smiled across the table at him.

"Tell me how you've been, Noah. Are you ready for school to start up again?"

"No, but I'm getting closer. I've been working on the bulletin boards in my classroom all this week. I can truthfully say I'd be happy if I never saw another letter template or scalloped border for the rest of my life."

Jess laughed. "You mean none of your enthusiastic female students have volunteered to help you?"

"Well, no. But Miss Summers in the English department did offer to loan me her electric stapler. Believe me, that's a hot commodity in the educational world. Oh, and the new assistant librarian baked me some cookies. It seems my image has changed quite a bit since you kissed me at the play."

She smiled. "I'm glad to hear that, Noah. It makes me feel as if I haven't been just a headache for you."

"I have no regrets, Jess." The look in his eyes reinforced his words. "I just wish we could've spent more time together, even if it was only as friends."

"You know what? I don't see why we still can't. God knows I don't like everything Lee does or everyone he associates with. He should know me well enough by now to trust me, so he can either accept our friendship or keep his opinion to himself. Either one works for me."

Noah looked wary but hopeful. "Are you sure, Jess? I'm not much of a pugilist."

She rolled her eyes. "You don't need to be, Noah. I'll make sure of that."

"Well, I'm game if you are. I'll take you any way I can get you." He started to take a sip of coffee and stopped with the mug halfway to his mouth. "Wait, that didn't come out right."

She laughed again. "Don't worry. I know what you meant."

They stayed and talked until Jess glanced at her watch and saw it was almost eight thirty. She didn't really expect Lee to call, but she wanted to be home in case he did. No sense agitating him unnecessarily.

"I guess I'd better get home," she said. "Some of us don't get the summer off and have to be at work early tomorrow."

He picked up their ticket and stood. "I should probably get to bed early myself since I'll be up late tomorrow night with the stargazers." He gave her a wistful smile. "I'm sorry you won't be there. It's supposed to be a clear night and promises to be a fabulous display."

Jess thought about it while he paid the cashier and made another bold decision as they walked to the car. "If you don't mind, Noah, I'd still like to go with you tomorrow night. It's not as if Lee would ever consider watching a meteor shower with me, so this could be my only chance."

His eyes lit up. "Of course I don't mind. We'll have a great time. And the rest of the stargazing club will be there too, so we'll have plenty of chaperones."

"Well, that's certainly a relief." She wiped a hand across her forehead. "Guess I can leave my pepper spray at home."

"I don't know about that," Noah said as he opened the car door for her. "Our club president is a rather lecherous eighty-year-old who'll probably offer to show you his Big Dipper."

She winced. "In that case, I'll be sticking close to you all night."

He took her hand to help her into the car. "I'll have to be sure and thank Luther for that."

****

Jess made it home by nine, but Lee didn't call. She considered phoning him at the Waldorf Astoria but decided against it after remembering the last time she'd called him at a hotel in New York.

She checked her e-mail and was thrilled to see a message from Cara, since she hadn't heard from her in a while. Cara said she'd found a TTM support group in Jacksonville that also held meetings for family members, so both her parents were attending with her. She was also happy about finding a hair salon in Jacksonville called California Trends where the stylists were sensitive to people with TTM and even specialized in hair extensions.

Over coffee the next morning at work, Jess told Deb about the fight with Lee and her decision to see Noah again. "I can't believe he thought he could forbid me to do something or dictate to me about my friends."

Deb nodded. "Yeah, he should know better than that since he hasn't been able to get rid of me. But it sounds like he got pretty mad about you seeing Noah anymore. Are you sure you want to provoke him with doing it again?"

"Excuse me?" Jess set down her coffee cup. "I expected you to be thrilled about anything that would burn Lee's butt."

"You know I'm always up for giving Lee hell," Deb said. "But are you sure it's smart to let Noah think he's still in the running if you've decided to stay married to the bonehead?"

"I don't think I'm doing that, Deb. Noah might still be hoping for more than friendship, but he knows that's all I'm offering. I made that clear, and he said he's fine with it."

"Are you sure, Jess? You said Lee's never been jealous of anybody like this before, so there must be something about Noah that makes him think he needs to be worried. Maybe Noah feels it too."

Jess thought about it a moment, then she shook her head. "If that's true, then they're both wrong. I really like Noah and don't see why I should have to give up a friend just because he's a man."

"I guess you're right." Deb took a sip of her coffee. "It's not Noah's fault you can't get over your unfortunate Lee affliction. Hey, maybe you can get a shot for it or something."

Jess gave her a wan smile. "No, I may as well face it that I'm a hopeless case. No matter what he does, I still love the jerk."

"Speaking of jerks, guess what Howie did." Deb's laugh sounded forced. "I gave him the whole spiel about my biological clock and all that kinda stuff, then I told him it was time for him to either fish or cut bait. Just my luck, he decided to abandon ship."

"What?" Jess frowned. "Stop with the bad nautical metaphors and tell me what happened. Did you break up?"

Deb shrugged and stared into her cup. "I haven't heard from him in two weeks, so I guess it means he chose his mother's cooking over me. How's that for a kick in the head? I lost out to cat-head biscuits and pecan pie."

Jess reached across the table and squeezed her hand. "Maybe he's just thinking it over."

"I don't think so, but it's fine with me anyway. Now I'm free to go after whoever they hire to replace Lee in the sports department. Guess I'll do like you and give the hunky-but-dumb type a try. What a sacrifice, huh?"

"I'm not buying the callous act, so you might as well drop it," Jess said. "Are you okay?"

Deb nodded. "I knew the risks of giving him an ultimatum. At least I can get on with my life now, right?"

"You're asking *me*? The one with the clueless, wandering husband I'm hooked on?" Jess sighed and they both stood up. "Hey, let's have lunch tomorrow and commiserate. We can go shopping in Atlanta too. What do you say?"

Deb smiled and put an arm around Jess's shoulders. "You definitely know my weaknesses, girlfriend. Nothing cheers me up more than eating and spending money."

Around mid-morning, Jess called home to check her messages, but there was still no word from Lee. She knew he'd been mad when he left, but he should've been over it by now and eager to tell her all the details of his new job whether she wanted to hear them or not. She couldn't help starting to worry about what he might have done in retribution for her defiance.

Her day's only high point was when she overheard a couple of the other sportswriters talking about a woman in New York who'd been arrested for trying to blackmail an ESPN reporter. Jess had already decided that she believed Lee's story, but now she knew for sure he'd been telling the truth.

When she finally got home at six, she went straight to check her answering machine and was relieved to see the message light flashing. But when she sat on the side of the bed and pressed the replay button, it wasn't Lee's voice she heard.

"Jessica, this is your mother. Please call me as soon as you get this message. It's very important."

Something about the way her mother sounded made Jess's heart speed up as she dialed her parents' number. When Marjorie answered, Jess could tell immediately that she was crying.

"Mother, what's wrong?"

"Oh, Jessica. Thank you so much for calling me back. I was afraid you still wouldn't want to talk to me."

"What happened, Mother? Why are you crying?"

"Your father's gone."

Jess gasped. "Oh my God! Daddy's dead?"

"No, of course not," Marjorie said. "He's left me, Jessica. For a thirty-year-old harlot who works in the country club pro shop!"

Jess managed to suppress a relieved sigh at the news of her father's continued survival. "Oh, Mother. I'm sure it's just some kind of misunderstanding. What did Daddy say?"

"He said, 'I'm divorcing you, Marjorie. I'm in love with another woman.' How much clearer could he have been?"

Jess listened to the sounds of Marjorie's crying and realized it was the first time she'd ever known her mother to shed a tear. She probably would have questioned the motive behind it if not for the real anguish that came through in her sobs. It hurt Jess just to hear it.

"I'm sorry, Mother. I wish there was something I could do to help. Do you want me to come home?"

"No—yes." Marjorie uttered a frustrated sigh. "I mean, I want you to come, but I can't ask you to do that. Especially after the way I treated you when you told me you were divorcing Lee. I wouldn't blame you if you hated me."

Jess's eyes widened, and she began to wonder if she was really talking to her mother or a skillful impersonator. "Don't be ridiculous, Mother. Of course I don't hate you. I'll leave for Tampa in the morning."

"Oh, Jessica, thank you for offering, but I'd rather be alone right now. I'm ashamed of making such an emotional spectacle of myself. I hope I can get it all out of my system over the weekend."

Jess couldn't help shaking her head at Marjorie's belief that she could get over the end of her thirty-year marriage in two days. "I don't like the idea of your being there alone, Mother. I really think I should come."

"I'd rather you didn't, dear. Really. I don't want anyone to see me this way."

"Well, all right. But call me if you change your mind and I'll come." Jess hesitated then asked, "Where's Daddy now?"

Marjorie sniffed. "He's staying with Elise and Garrett—can you believe that? I suppose Elise is worried about Garrett's future with your father's company if she doesn't take his side in this. You've been right about her all along, Jessica. She's a spoiled brat and thinks only of herself."

Jess didn't recall ever expressing those particular sentiments about her sister, but she couldn't help taking a little guilty pleasure in hearing them come from her mother. She would of course have to call Elise later and get her father's side of the story, but she saw no reason to mention that to Marjorie now. Elise had been the Good Daughter all her life. It was Jess's turn for a while.

She listened to her mother's account of how her father had gone to work that morning, cleaned out his desk and told his secretary he was finally starting his retirement. Then he'd gone to the country club and spent the day playing golf and getting "snockered" as Marjorie described it. When he finally came home, he'd told Marjorie that life was too short for him to live any longer with a woman who either berated him or ignored him, and he'd finally found someone who made him happy. He'd packed his bags and told Marjorie he would be staying with Elise and Garrett until he found a place of his own.

"And before he left," Marjorie said, "he had the audacity to tell me he wished me the best and hoped I'd be happy someday. If he cared one iota about my happiness, he wouldn't be deserting me like this!"

"But, Mother, did you really think of your marriage as happy?" Jess asked.

"Of course I did. Your father and I got along well and never fought. Wouldn't you consider that happy?"

"Not really. And I have to admit I'd always wondered what had attracted you and Daddy to each other in the first place. You didn't seem to have anything in common." Jess didn't want to invite her mother's wrath, but she also wasn't willing to be dishonest just to stay on her good side.

"Your father was extremely handsome and charming as a young man," Marjorie said. "I'd think you'd understand that kind of attraction better than most women, Jessica, considering your own husband."

"Well, yes I do, but there has to be more to a relationship than just…the physical side of it." Was she really having this conversation with her mother?

"Good heavens, I'm not talking about *sex*. I wanted an attractive, responsible man who would provide for me and be the father of my children, and Bill was perfect for the job. We always managed to work around our differences and make compromises for personal pursuits. I don't know why he has to change everything now after all these years."

Jess remembered something Marjorie had said once about men being discreet. "Mother, are you saying that Daddy had affairs in the past that you knew about?"

"I'm saying he always managed to keep anything he did in perspective and not let it disrupt our life. I can only assume he's going through some kind of midlife crisis right now that's making him act so foolishly over this woman." Marjorie paused to blow her nose. "The very idea of a man his age talking about such nonsense as *love*."

Jess realized she had never heard her parents say they loved each other, nor could she remember ever hearing her mother talk about love at all. Before she could stop herself, she asked Marjorie the question that was foremost in her mind.

"Have you ever been in love, Mother?"

"What a thing to ask me," Marjorie said. "And

what does that have to do with any of this?"

Jess knew their tenuous bond was in grave danger if the conversation continued much longer, but she honestly felt bad for her mother and wanted to know the truth. Maybe she could help her if they were honest with each other.

"Everyone needs love in their life, Mother. Who we love and why we love them is sometimes hard to understand, but if I've learned anything from the problems I've had with Lee, it's that there's no substitute for the happiness that only comes from being with the one person in the world whose heart speaks the same language as yours."

Jess held her breath in anticipation of her mother's angry response, but she released it in surprise seconds later when she heard soft crying sounds again.

"We aren't all lucky enough to find something like that, Jessica. And some of us are afraid we're either too old or too jaded to recognize it if we ever did. Or even worse"—Marjorie paused to sniff again—"that the closest we'll ever get to love has just walked out on us."

"If Daddy's not the right person for you, then you both deserve the chance to keep looking. And don't worry. You'll know when you find them, because your heart won't let you give up on them no matter how hard you try to do it. Believe me, I know."

"Is that why you took Lee back?"

Tears streamed down Jess's cheeks because her mother hadn't automatically assumed that it had been Lee who'd taken *her* back.

"Yes. He's arrogant, self-centered, and clueless ninety percent of the time, but the other ten percent is why I'll always love him."

Marjorie sighed. "I can't imagine how you got to be so wise about matters of the heart with a wretch like me for a mother. I'm sorry I didn't give you any support when I was there—about your marriage or anything else. I promise I'll do better in the future if you can forgive me."

"Thank you, Mother." Jess smiled through her tears. "I hope we can both be there for each other from now on, and I'd like to start by coming to see you this weekend. I'll wait until tomorrow to leave so you'll have tonight to be by yourself and recoup. Okay?"

Marjorie agreed, and after Jess hung up the phone, she lay on the bed and marveled at how her parents' divorce could actually be such a blessing in disguise for her relationship with her mother. And she wished Lee were there so she could talk to him about it, because he knew better than anyone how much it meant to her.

The things she'd said to her mother about always loving Lee were the truth. Given the choice between a loveless but congenial marriage like her parents had and the passionate turbulence she and Lee shared, Jess would definitely keep what she had. She decided to swallow her pride and call him in the morning if he hadn't called her by then.

She was in the middle of making herself a loaded baked potato the way she loved them—with bacon, sour cream, salsa, and three kinds of cheese—when the phone rang and she almost trampled poor Ming in her rush to answer it, hoping it was Lee. She tried not to let the disappointment show in her voice when it was Noah.

"Sorry to bother you, Jess, but I'm calling to see if I can pick you up a little earlier than eleven o'clock tonight."

"Well, sure, Noah." She bent to smooth Ming's ruffled fur. "How much earlier?"

"Would eight be a problem?"

"No, but is something wrong? You sound a little odd."

He laughed. "New uncle jitters, I guess. My sister-in-law is about to deliver my first niece or nephew."

"Oh, how exciting. Are you at the hospital now?"

"No, that's why I need to pick you up early. Would you mind helping me select an appropriate gift for the baby and going to the hospital with me?"

She smiled. "Of course I don't mind. We can't have you presenting the newborn with a copy of Washington's biography or a lock of Hamilton's hair."

"Drat, there go my two best ideas."

Jess laughed. "I figured as much. See you at eight."

Chapter Eighteen

When Jess finished eating her scrumptious potato, she got dressed for her stargazing date with Noah and opted for jeans and a long-sleeved T-shirt so she wouldn't have to take a jacket. While giving her hair a once-over, she scowled at an unruly lock at her right temple and struggled to resist lopping it off. She heard Noah at the front door right before giving in.

"Saved by the bell," she told her obstinate tresses as she put down the scissors, making a mental note to let Lee pick the hiding place the next time she hid them from herself. She snickered on the way to the door and greeted Noah with a wry smile.

"Come in and sit down for a minute," she said. "I'm not quite ready."

"There's actually no hurry now." He followed her to the living room. "My brother called just before I left and said the contractions have stalled, so it might be tomorrow before the baby gets here. I thought we could just get some coffee and pie to kill time before we go to the environmental center."

"Ooh, that sounds good. I've been dying for some key lime pie." When Ming jumped onto Noah's lap as soon as he sat down, Jess shook her head. "If you'll indulge my cat in a little flirting while I get my purse, we can go."

"No problem." He scratched Ming under the chin.

"Her adoration is good for my ego."

When Jess returned to the living room a few minutes later, she said, "Do the doctors know what caused your sister-in-law's labor to slow down? I hope there's no danger to the baby."

Noah placed Ming on the couch beside him and stood up. "My brother said it's common with first babies, but they're monitoring her closely for complications."

"Do you have a cell phone so he can call you?"

He shook his head. "I hate those things and refuse to get one."

"I don't like them either, but I had to get one because of my job. Unfortunately, it needs a new battery and won't do us any good right now." Jess thought a minute, then she put a hand on his arm. "I know you're worried about them, so why don't you call the hospital and give your brother my number here? He can leave you a message on my answering machine if anything changes, and we can check my messages from a pay phone while we're out."

Noah looked relieved. "Thanks, Jess. That'll help ease my mind a lot."

She showed him the extension in the hall and went to make sure the answering machine was turned on while he called his brother. He was smiling when she returned to the living room.

"He said the doctor just gave her something that's supposed to make the contractions start up again. He'll call in half an hour or so and leave a message to let me know if it worked, so I might become an uncle tonight after all."

"Oh, good," Jess said. "Do you want to stay here

and wait for his call?"

"No," he said with a little laugh. "Since you mentioned that key lime pie, I seem to have a taste for it myself. We can check your messages from the coffee shop and go to the hospital from there if anything's happening."

"Okay, then let's go."

Halfway down the sidewalk on the way to the car, Ming darted between them and Jess realized she had followed them out the door.

"Ming, you bad girl! Get back in the house."

"Don't scold her, Jess. She just can't bear to see me go."

Noah bent to pick up the cowering feline at the same instant that Ollie, the dachshund from next door, charged toward them in a barking frenzy. Ming hissed once then raced across the lawn toward a sycamore tree in the middle of the next yard with Ollie in the hottest pursuit his stubby little legs would allow.

"Ollie, you stop chasing that cat!" Mrs. Lamm shouted from her porch. "You know the vet said not to overexert yourself!"

Ming scampered up the tree and took refuge on a limb about twelve feet off the ground, her blue eyes glittering in terror. Jess managed to pick up the yapping dachshund and carry him to his frantic owner while Noah tried to coax Ming from the tree.

"She's not budging," he said when Jess came back. "And I can't quite reach her. Do you have a ladder?"

"I have a stepstool in the kitchen. You might be able to reach her with that."

She ran back into the house for the stool and got an idea while she was there. When she returned, Mrs.

Lamm had put the dog inside and joined Noah under the tree.

"Ollie wouldn't have hurt her, you know," the woman was telling Noah as Jess walked up. "He loves cats and just wanted to play."

"I don't think she knows that," Noah said. "She must not speak dachshund."

Mrs. Lamm laughed. "Sure is nice of you to help Jess with her cat. Lord knows that husband of hers wouldn't concern himself about it. Why, do you know he once told me he thinks that cat is 'the devil incarcerated'? I suppose he meant *incarnate*, but what a thing to say either way."

"She's clearly a feline of discriminating tastes." Noah gave Jess an amused look. "If only her mistress held all the same opinions."

Jess elbowed him. "Here's the stool, and I brought a sardine for an enticement." She held up the little fishy by the tail.

"That wasn't necessary, Jess." Noah wrinkled his nose as he stepped up on the stool. "I'll get her down for nothing."

"He's a funny one, ain't he?" Mrs. Lamm eyed Noah appreciatively. "And a tall drink of water too."

Ming was still a few inches out of Noah's reach, so he turned to Jess and extended his hand. "Let me try the sardine." He held it up to Ming and as soon as she got a whiff of it, she jumped into his arms and seized the fish in her mouth, tearing into it with vigor against his chest.

"Oh, Noah, I'm so sorry." Jess tried to stifle her laughter. "I forgot she always eats them like that."

"No problem." He wiped ineffectively at the oily spot on the front of his shirt.

"You need to rub some baking soda on that before you wash it," Mrs. Lamm volunteered. "Unless you want to walk around smelling like *eau de fish*."

They thanked her for the laundry tip, then Jess and Noah went back inside. When he put Ming down, she walked imperiously into the living room and jumped onto the coffee table to wash her face as if nothing out of the ordinary had taken place. Jess watched her with amused exasperation, then she gave Noah's arm a grateful squeeze.

"Thank you for your help. I feel terrible about your shirt."

"Don't give it another thought."

"Well, you can't go to the hospital like this. Take it off and let me see what I can do with it."

He took a step back. "Oh, that's not necessary. It'll be fine."

"Nonsense, Noah." Jess began unbuttoning his shirt. "You can't visit a newborn smelling like fish. I'd give you something else to wear if I could, but all Lee's shirts—" She broke off and concentrated on his buttons. "It won't take long to run this through a quick wash and dry cycle. I'll make us some coffee while we wait, and I think I even have some cheesecake."

"Well, all right." His face was as red as Jess's hair, but he took off the shirt and handed it to her. "There's no need to wash the undershirt. I'll keep it on."

"Okay, that's probably a good idea," she said with a mischievous smile. "I'm not sure Ming and I can be trusted around you otherwise."

His blush deepened, but he laughed. "I might believe that in Ming's case."

She stopped off in the kitchen to start the coffee

brewing and to get the baking soda per Mrs. Lamm's advice. Then she took the shirt to the utility room off the garage and put it in the washer. When she returned to the kitchen, she heard Noah's voice in the living room and went to see if he was talking to his brother on the phone.

Her heart lurched as soon as she saw the look on his face, afraid it was bad news about the baby. But when he held out the receiver to her and mouthed a silent apology with eyes full of remorse, she realized who was on the phone. She closed her eyes as she put the receiver to her ear.

"Lee, it's not what you think."

"Save it, Jess." Fury was audible in his voice. "Go ahead and sleep with him if that's what you want so much. I'll give you your damn divorce as soon as I get back!"

"Lee, wait—"

The line went dead. Jess stared at the phone in her hand as if it would explain Lee's ridiculous reaction, then the room suddenly began to spin. She felt sure she would have hit the floor and given herself a concussion if Noah hadn't been there to steady her. She leaned against him a moment, waiting for the vertigo to disappear, and he put a tentative arm around her.

"Jess, I'm so sorry. If I'd known—"

"It's not your fault, Noah."

"Are you all right? What did he say?"

She couldn't help her mirthless laugh. "This is just too ironic for words. I threw him out because a woman answered the phone in his hotel room, and now he wants a divorce because you answered our phone. And we both jumped to the wrong conclusions."

"I'm sure it's not as bad as you think," Noah said. "I'll tell him I came over uninvited if you want me to."

She looked up at him and shook her head. "Thank you, but he's probably too mad for it to make any difference. And you shouldn't have to lie anyway, because we haven't done anything wrong. I have no idea why he'd suddenly think I would ever be unfaithful when he knows me better than that, but I'll tell him nothing happened when he gets back. There's no reason for him not to believe me."

Noah didn't say anything for a moment, then he sighed. "Jess, you'd know I was lying if I said I didn't wish we could be more than friends, but I hope you believe that I want you to be happy more than anything else. I don't understand why you want to stay with a man who doesn't seem right for you and either can't or won't give you everything you deserve, but I truly hope things will work out for the two of you if you're sure that's what you really want. And I care about you too much not to be your friend regardless."

She was so glad she hadn't abandoned this sweet man's friendship, even though it had possibly just cost her her marriage.

"Thank you, Noah. And I think maybe this meteor shower tonight could be some sort of cosmic gift to us. What do you say we go wish on a few falling stars?"

He smiled and took her hands. "Okay, but I don't think we'll be wishing for the same things."

"But that's not our concern, is it? Wishers only make the wishes. It's up to God or Fate or the Wizard of Oz to decide which ones should come true. All we can do is wish for our heart's true desire and hope for the best."

Chapter Nineteen

After an hour-long wait at the hospital, Noah got to meet his nephew, Joshua Noah Hamilton. He gave his sister-in-law a hug and proudly presented her with the gifts Jess had helped him select: a silver-plated picture frame and an uncirculated coin set for the baby's birth year. Considering Noah's esteem for Alexander Hamilton who'd been the nation's first treasury secretary, Jess could tell he was partial to the latter gift.

They arrived at the environmental center a little before eleven thirty. Noah introduced Jess to the other stargazers and their notorious president, Luther Cox. When Jess shook Luther's hand, his grip belied his frail appearance.

"Dadgum, boy," Luther said to Noah. "You did *good*. Is this the librarian that's been baking cookies for you or the one with the mouth-breather for a husband?"

Even in the dark, Jess could see Noah's blush. "Luther, I…uh…"

"Never mind." Luther linked Jess's arm with his. "Darlin', come sit over here next to me where it's nice and dark. I've been making the ladies see stars for eighty years, and I can guarantee you'll forget all about books or husbands or whatever it is you might have on your mind."

"Thank you, Luther." Jess extracted her arm with more than a little effort. "But I'm Noah's date tonight.

Besides, my mother always warned me about boys and dark places."

"Well, suit yourself, Red." Luther hitched his trousers a little closer to his armpits. "I'll be over by the fishpond if you get bored with Junior here."

"Luther," Noah said, "isn't that Mrs. Thatcher standing over there by the telescope? I'm glad to see she's finally getting out again since Mr. Thatcher passed away last spring."

Luther peered over his spectacles at the lady in question. "Hmm…I think you're right, boy. Reckon I'd best go welcome her back. Presidential duties and all, you know."

Jess laughed as she helped Noah set up the lounge chairs they'd brought. "I guess he's proof that old playboys never die. They just trade in their sports cars for motorized scooters."

"He's harmless really," Noah said. "He was married for sixty years and was so devastated when his wife died two years ago that we were afraid he'd soon follow her from grief. We were all relieved when he decided to take up lechery as a hobby."

They got situated on their respective chairs, and Jess reached over to touch Noah's arm. "You're such a caring man. You don't just make acquaintances, you're a real friend to everyone you know."

"Thank you, Jess. Your opinion means a lot to me." He cleared his throat before adding, "Sorry about that mouth-breather comment."

She had to laugh. "Don't let it bother you, Noah. I don't blame you for seeing Lee that way, considering how he's acted around you. But he's not always such a lout. He may be the Master of Malaprops and like to run all his metaphors through a blender, but he's not dumb by any means. And he has a real talent for writing about sports."

"Really?" Noah sounded genuinely surprised.

Jess nodded. "He has a knack for injecting excitement and humor into his stories without resorting to the cheesy clichés a lot of other sportswriters use. The enthusiasm comes through because Lee genuinely loves sports himself, and it shows in his writing. He also understands the athletes' emotions, and that helps him bring out the human side of his stories."

Noah gave her a intent look. "He's lucky to have someone like you who understands and appreciates him. It's a shame he doesn't give you the same things in return. You deserve a better man than that."

Although Jess had thought the same thing before and had been trying to get Lee to see it for the past few months, she felt defensive at the criticism of him.

"That's not fair, Noah. You've only seen him at his worst and don't really know him."

"True, but I've known other men like him. My father for one." Noah's features took on a hardened cast that Jess wouldn't have believed possible if she wasn't seeing it for herself.

"How do you mean?"

He sighed after a few seconds of silence. "When you met my brother at the hospital, I'm sure you noticed the differences between us. He got our father's athletic build and talent for sports, and I—to my father's immense and oft-stated disappointment—took after my mother's intellectual side of the family."

The bitterness in his voice was so plain that Jess wasn't sure she should pursue the subject, but her curiosity won out. "I did notice the difference, but I could also see how close you and your brother are."

"You're right, we're very close. Fortunately, he only took after our father physically and didn't inherit his temper and lack of morals."

"I'm sorry, Noah. It's hard to imagine anyone as sweet as you having a father like that."

"Actually, I'd think you'd understand it better than most people, Jess."

She drew back a little in surprise. "Why would you say that?"

He looked a bit hesitant, but he said, "Because you're married to a man who cheated on you and uses his fists to solve his problems."

Jess probably would have been angry if she hadn't been so confused by where all this was coming from. "Neither of those things is true. Lee had an explanation for what happened in New York, and he only threatened to hit you. I don't believe he would have done it."

Noah nodded. "My mother has always refused to believe the truth about my father too, but I know better. That's why I didn't want to see you make the same mistakes and felt I had to do something about it."

"What do you mean?"

"Jess, I have a confession to make." He paused to take a deep breath. "When I saw your husband that night after you left the lecture, I decided I wasn't going to let him intimidate me the way I did the first time—the way I'd always let my father bully me when I was growing up because I didn't fit his image of what a man is supposed to be. But since I'm neither foolish enough nor barbaric enough to fight your husband physically, I had to fight him on another level."

Jess frowned. "What did you do?"

"I…I led him to believe you and I were a couple back in high school, and I told him the only thing that kept us from sleeping together the night we had dinner was the delay he'd been causing in your divorce."

Lee's rage and behavior suddenly made perfect sense.

"Oh my God. No wonder he had such a fit about me seeing you again."

Noah's eyes were full of remorse. "Jess, I'm sorry I was dishonest, but I truly felt I was doing it for your own good. I thought maybe it would make him stop stalling and let you go."

"Why in the world would you think that, Noah? Didn't you realize it would only make him even more determined to stop you?"

"No, I really didn't expect that. I thought it would make him see that you were serious about the divorce so he would give it to you. Either that or…" He lowered his gaze to the ground between them.

"Or what, Noah?"

"Or it would make him mad enough to hit me, and you wouldn't forgive him for doing it."

"To be honest, I can't believe he *didn't* hit you. I'm almost proud of him for showing that much restraint."

He still didn't look at her. "Does that mean you want to hit me yourself?"

She laughed and reached over to put a hand on his arm again. "Of course not. I'm even less of a pugilist than you are. Besides, you're a lot bigger than me."

He raised his head with a relieved smile. "Can you forgive me?"

"There's really nothing to forgive. Like I said, you

probably just spurred him to try even harder with me. And it certainly doesn't hurt for him to know I'm not oblivious to every other man in the world besides him."

"He should've already known he has a wife other men would love to steal. Is he really that dense, or is it just too much vanity?"

"Oh, he's definitely vain enough for three people, but I can't really fault him for that. It's not as if he doesn't have a reason to be."

"But don't you need more than that in a man?"

She didn't know why she still wasn't angry with him for lying to Lee, but his question didn't bother her a bit. In fact, it made her want to talk to him about it.

"Yes, I do, and that's what I was trying to make him understand while we were separated. For a while, I was afraid there wasn't anything between us but physical attraction. And even when I decided to try again with him, it was because I thought I loved him enough that nothing else should matter. But maybe I was wrong."

"Why do you say that?" Jess didn't miss the hopeful note in his voice. "You mean you aren't sure you should have taken him back, or you aren't sure you love him?"

She looked up at the sky as if she might find an answer amongst the stars. "No, the *only* thing I'm sure of is that I love him. I'm just afraid I lost all chance at getting through to him when I gave in and let him come back home. That he'll keep doing whatever he wants because he knows he can get away with it. Of course, none of this will matter if we can't get past this fight about you."

"Are you saying it might be a good thing if he does

want a divorce?"

She sighed. "No, I don't think I'd ever call it a good thing, but I'm starting to wonder if it might be unavoidable."

"Is there anything I can do to help convince you that you're right?"

She looked at him with a rueful smile. "Oh, I think you've done quite enough, Mr. Hamilton."

"Well, I don't agree." He moved his chair over so that it was touching hers, then he sat down again and put his arm around her. "I think I should strike a blow for all the nice guys in the world who never got their picture in the sports section of the newspaper. Besides, you told me to stick close to you tonight, remember?"

"You're right," she said with a little laugh. And his arm did feel nice behind her. "I guess you can keep me warm while you protect me from Luther."

"My pleasure," he said, pulling her closer. "And I know exactly what to wish for now."

"Noah, am I going to need that pepper spray after all?"

"I certainly hope so," he replied, and they both laughed.

Jess looked up at the sky and saw her first meteor, its exceptionally bright trail visible for at least two seconds. She closed her eyes to make the wish she intended to make as many times as possible over the course of the night: that everything would work out for the best, whatever that turned out to be.

****

The phone woke her at seven the next morning.

"Get your lazy butt out of bed and get dressed!" Deb said. "You'll never guess what happened!"

Jess yawned and stretched. "You're right. I'll never guess, so tell me."

"Howie proposed! To *me*."

Jess sat up and squealed into the phone like a sixth grader. "When, how, and where?"

"Last night, on one knee, in my living room. He also moved out of his mother's house and got an apartment in Stoneridge, and he wants me to move in with him. He said we've already wasted too much time. Can you believe it, girlfriend?"

"Deb, that's wonderful! I told you Howie would come through for you."

"Can you come help me get packed up and moved today? I want to hurry before he gets his body back from the pod people."

Jess laughed. "Of course I'll help you. I have to go see my mother in Tampa today, but I'll be back in the morning and can come help you then if you still need me."

"Oh, I will. Howie has the truck reserved for tomorrow. Today we're packing."

"Okay, I'll call you when I get back. And I'll see if Noah can help us so you can meet him. He lives in Stoneridge too."

"Oh, great. I'm sure that'll go over big with El Jerko."

Jess looked at Ming curled up beside her on Lee's pillow. "That might be a moot point."

"Why? What happened?"

"Uh-uh," Jess said. "It's a long, sad story, and I don't want to depress you with it when we're supposed to be celebrating your happiness. I'll tell you about it when I get back and we get you all moved in with

Howie."

After she hung up with Deb, Jess called Noah to see if he'd help, and he said he'd volunteer to move pianos if it meant he got to see her again. She hung up wondering once more why she couldn't have fallen in love with a sweet man like Noah instead of losing her heart to El Jerko.

She'd swallowed her pride and called Lee's cell phone when she got home from the environmental center around two, but the call had gone straight to voice mail. Even though she'd known it would probably be futile, she'd gotten the number for the Waldorf Astoria from the Internet and called his room. No answer there either. She hadn't bothered to leave a message, but when the phone rang just as she was about to leave for Tampa, she ran to catch it in case it was Lee.

"Hey, Jess. It's Trent."

She could tell from his voice that he wasn't calling just to shoot the bull. "Hey, Trent. What's wrong?"

"I, uh…got a call from Lee last night. He didn't sound too good."

"What did he say?" Jess sat on the bed with her hand on her forehead.

"He was pretty wasted and didn't make much sense, but he made me promise to come over there and get his stuff for him. He said he…didn't want to see you. I'm sorry, Jess."

What little hope she'd had that Lee would cool off before he came home disappeared. "It's not your fault, Trent."

"Listen, Jess. I don't know what's going on between you two, but I hope this doesn't have anything to do with that stuff that happened in New York the first time he went. I can't tell you how many women he turned down while he was staying here with me, and he told me you were the only woman in the world for him. I know he'd never cheat on you."

She knew it too, but it didn't matter anymore. In keeping with her penchant for irony, now she was the one who needed someone to vouch for her fidelity.

"This doesn't have anything to do with not trusting him, but thanks for telling me that, Trent. I'm glad to know he's got such a good friend looking out for him."

"No problem, Jess. Look, I can't make it over there until after five tomorrow when I get off. Will you be home then?"

"Probably not, but I can stop by the gym tomorrow and give you my extra key before you get off. You're right down the street from Stoneridge apartments, right?"

"Yeah, about three blocks north. Thanks, Jess. You're a class act."

She didn't feel very classy while she drove to Tampa with tears rolling down her cheeks. She also wondered how much she should tell Marjorie about it all when she saw her since she didn't want to whine about her own problems when she was supposed to be there to support her mother. On the other hand, maybe they could connect even more over their shared marriage troubles. She had always envied her friends who were close to their moms.

So despite her worries, Jess drove home with an undeniable sense of elation at the prospect of having her first real heart-to-heart talk with her own mother.

Chapter Twenty

Jess found her mother sitting on the back deck, watching the boats out on Hillsborough Bay with a pitcher of margaritas on the table in front of her. Marjorie got up to hug her daughter as soon as she saw her.

"Thank you for coming, Jessica. It's so good to see you. Go to the kitchen and get the glass I put in the freezer for you. I want you to join me in a toast."

"A toast to what?" Something had definitely brought about a major improvement in her mother's frame of mind.

"To *freedom*, my dear." Marjorie drained her glass and refilled it. "Freedom and new beginnings."

When Jess returned from the kitchen with her frosted, pre-salted glass, Marjorie filled it then held her own glass aloft.

"Here's to the rest of our life's journey, and to finding the best route for reaching our destination." Marjorie clinked their glasses together.

Jess took a sip. "I'm glad to see you in such high spirits, Mother. I think it's exactly what we both need right now."

"I couldn't agree more." Marjorie motioned for Jess to sit in one of the other patio chairs. "But why do you sound so glum, dear? Was Lee upset with you for leaving him alone to come console your poor mother?"

Jess touched the salt crystals on the rim of her glass. "I don't think Lee cares what I do anymore."

Marjorie put her hand over Jess's. "Tell me what happened. As you can see, I'm over my moping and don't need you to coddle me. I want you to tell me what's wrong between you and Lee, and I want you to start from the beginning."

Jess could tell from her expression that both her interest and concern were genuine. She told her the whole sordid story, beginning with the convention in New York and ending with Lee's phone call to Trent. By the time she finished, the margarita pitcher was empty and Jess actually felt more giggly than weepy.

"Do you think he's serious about wanting a divorce?" Marjorie asked. "It doesn't make sense after all the effort he put into fighting it when you wanted one."

"I know, but I learned a long time ago not to expect Lee to make sense," Jess replied. "Besides, this time his precious male ego is on the line. He thinks I've been doing the horizontal hokey-pokey with Noah." She snickered and drained the last few drops from her glass.

Marjorie rolled her eyes. "Good heavens. Why do men always think sex is as much of a big deal to us as it is to them?"

Jess blinked and hesitated only a second before saying, "It *is* a big deal to me, Mother. He's not wrong about that. It's just that he should know I'd never do it with anyone but him." She was relieved when Marjorie looked surprised rather than shocked.

"Honestly, Jessica? I've never quite understood the draw of it myself."

"Trust me, Mother. If performed correctly with the

209

right person, it's a *gargantuan* deal."

"Hmm…" Marjorie said. "Then perhaps I'll add it to my list of things to explore on my upcoming journey. I may even move it ahead of skydiving."

They both laughed, and Jess got up to hug her mother. "I'm so glad you're looking at all this as a positive, Mother. I can't help feeling it's the best thing for both you and Daddy."

Marjorie returned the hug then held Jess at arm's length. "I hope you're right. I had a long talk with myself last night, and I decided I still have plenty of life left to live. And I don't need a husband in order to do it."

"Good for you." Jess sat down beside Marjorie. "And you're absolutely right. You're still young and have a lot of living to do."

Marjorie picked up her glass and twirled the stem between her fingers. "Yes, and after the past few weeks I've just had, I appreciate my remaining years a lot more."

"Have things been bad between you and Daddy?"

Marjorie continued to look at the glass in her hands. "No, he was actually quite supportive until it was all over."

Jess frowned. "What do you mean, Mother?"

"My doctor saw something on my last mammogram that concerned him. He sent me for a follow-up ultrasound, and they found a mass. I got the results of the biopsy Thursday afternoon, and it turned out to be a benign cyst. To your father's credit, he was with me when I got the news. At least he stuck around long enough to make sure I wasn't dying before he left me."

"Oh my God, Mother. Why didn't you tell me any of this was going on?"

"I didn't want to say anything about it until I knew for sure what I was dealing with. And I certainly couldn't expect you to come hold my hand while I had the tests done considering the way I acted when you told me about your illness." Marjorie put a hand on her forehead and sighed. "It's no wonder you pull out your hair with a mother like me."

Jess took her hand down and held it in both of hers. "My disorder is no more your fault than it would be if I had diabetes. And please don't ever keep anything to do with your health from me again. I happen to like holding your hand."

Marjorie smiled and hugged her again. "I like it too, Jessica. And in the future, I intend to make quite a few changes to the way I do everything. Last night while I was pulling myself out of the vat of self pity I'd fallen into, I decided that this reminder of my mortality was a wakeup call to let me know I needed to take a good look at my life. And that I needed to fix all the things that desperately needed fixing."

"That's wonderful, Mother. I'm proud of you for turning all this into something positive."

"Thank you, dear. But I have to wonder if your separation from Lee couldn't be just as positive for you. Don't you have things you've always wanted to do that you've put aside because of your marriage?"

"Well, there is one thing. I've always wanted to do some writing of my own."

"You mean newspaper articles?"

"No, I mean fiction." Jess suspected the margaritas were responsible for her candor, because she didn't hesitate to add, "I have a few short stories I've written, and I think—no, I know at least one of them is good enough to be published."

Marjorie's eyes lit up. "How wonderful, Jessica. I've always thought your talent was wasted in that little copyediting job. I definitely think you should pursue this."

Jess could only stare at her for a moment. "Thank you, Mother. It means a lot to me that you think I can do it."

"I might even be able to help you," Marjorie said. "I happen to belong to the same country club as the father-in-law of a successful author who lives here in Tampa. I'm sure he'd be happy to introduce you to her if I ask him. I'll call and see if they can meet us for lunch at the club this afternoon."

"Oh, no, Mother." Jess shook her head emphatically. "I'd be petrified to meet a real author. Besides, it's too much of an imposition."

"Nonsense." Marjorie waved away Jess's protest as she stood up. "It's about time all the pretentious socializing I've always done served a useful purpose. I'll get my address book and call him right now."

Jess had never been overly fond of her parents' country club acquaintances, and the prospect of talking about her amateur writing efforts with a published author was more than a little daunting. But her mother's enthusiasm about helping filled her with a joy she'd never felt before, and there was no way she could turn down her offer to help.

Marjorie came back to the deck and told Jess everything was set. They had just enough time to freshen up before they needed to leave for the country club. Jess went upstairs and decided she definitely needed a shower to help clear her head of the margaritas' effects. When she finished dressing, she went to her mother's bedroom and sat on the bed while Marjorie applied her makeup.

"I really can't imagine both of them being able to meet us on such short notice, Mother. I hope you didn't bully them into this."

Marjorie laughed. "I'm flattered that you think I'm persuasive enough to accomplish something like that, but I can assure you that no one bullies Mack Stanton into anything. He's one of the most prominent businessmen in the state of Florida." She paused to apply her lipstick. "And one of the most handsome as well."

"Oh, really?" Jess met her mother's gaze in the mirror and smiled. "Could there be an ulterior motive for you in this meeting?"

"Nonsense, dear. His charm and good looks are merely fringe benefits."

"Is he married?"

"Not that it matters, but I believe he's a widower. And stop smiling at me like that, Jessica."

Jess's smile widened. "You must know him pretty well to ask for something like this out of the blue. What's the scoop, Mother?"

"There is no *scoop*." Marjorie added a spritz of hairspray to her flawless blonde curls and looked at Jess in the mirror. "I simply knew Mack was playing in the golf tournament at the club this weekend, so I called and asked him if his daughter-in-law might be able to join us there for lunch so you could meet her. He was delighted with the idea."

Jess's eyes narrowed. "By any chance, is Daddy also playing in this golf tournament?"

"I have no idea and couldn't possibly care less. Why do you ask?"

"Oh, I don't know. I just wonder what Daddy will think if he sees you having lunch with a wealthy, handsome widower. That hadn't crossed your mind at all, Mother?"

Marjorie managed to keep a straight face for an impressive three seconds. "Your father *detests* Mack Stanton." She turned around and put a hand on Jess's knee. "I hope Bill sees us and it makes him inhale the olive from his martini."

Jess laughed as she stood up. "Well, since he's my father and I love him, I'll have to save him with the Heimlich maneuver if he chokes. But I don't blame you for hoping it."

"That's fair enough, dear. Just make sure the olive hits his girlfriend in the eye when it pops out."

On the drive to the country club, Marjorie told Jess that Mack's daughter-in-law had published a successful anthology of children's stories, and she also had a highly popular series of children's books about a feisty ten-year-old heroine who takes on everyone from her alcoholic father to an insidious pedophile preying on one of her friends.

When they entered the country club's dining room, the hostess greeted them with an ingratiating smile. "Good afternoon, Mrs. Hunter. Mr. Stanton is waiting for you and your daughter at his regular table."

"Thank you, Clarice," Marjorie said. "I know where it is."

Jess followed her mother to a table by the window

at which sat an exceptionally handsome older gentleman of at least sixty. He stood when he saw them approaching, and Jess thought he had one of the most spectacular smiles she'd ever seen. It even rivaled Lee's.

"Marjorie, you get lovelier every time I see you." He surprised Jess by bending to kiss her mother's hand. "And you can't possibly expect me to believe this beautiful young woman is your daughter unless you had her at the age of ten." He continued to hold Marjorie's hand as he smiled at Jess.

"Mack, you're a shameless liar, but I'll forgive you." Marjorie's cheeks flushed like a schoolgirl's. "This is my daughter, Jessica Cassady."

"Delighted to meet you, Jessica," Mack said as he shook her hand. "My daughter-in-law will be joining us shortly. She said to tell you she's looking forward to meeting you and talking about your writing."

"Thank you for making time for us on such short notice, Mr. Stanton," Jess said as they took their seats.

"It was no trouble at all," he said. "And please call me Mack. I was thrilled that Marjorie finally accepted my invitation to lunch after turning me down for so many years."

Jess watched him give her mother a look that brought another flush to Marjorie's cheeks, and she understood exactly why her father disliked this man so much. She also felt as if she were getting a preview of what Lee would look like in about thirty years, and she had to smile despite the stab of pain she felt as she wondered if they'd still be together then.

"As I told you on the phone, Mack," Marjorie said, "quite a few circumstances have changed for me recently. Taking an interest in Jessica's writing is just one of the positive changes I intend to make."

"Splendid news on all accounts." He touched Marjorie's hand briefly before turning his attention to Jess. "What kind of writing do you do, my dear?"

"I'm a copyeditor for a small newspaper in Georgia, but I have a few short stories I've written and revised a ridiculous number of times."

"You must be a perfectionist. Quite an admirable quality, in my opinion." He looked up as a couple approached their table. "Ah, here are my son and daughter-in-law now."

Jess turned and could see that good looks definitely ran in the Stanton family, because the man was a younger, much darker version of his father. He had one arm wrapped rather possessively around the waist of a blonde woman whose voluptuous figure had the attention of all the men in the room and drew disdainful looks from most of the women.

Mack stood to take his daughter-in-law's hand when they reached the table. "Jaycee, my dear. Thank you for coming. This is my good friend Marjorie Hunter and her daughter, Jessica."

"It's good to meet you." Jaycee shook their hands. "This is my husband Bud, but he's not staying because he has a date with our daughter at the wedding photographer's."

Bud greeted Jess and Marjorie then turned to his father. "Keep an eye on her, Dad. She's still on probation here from the last incident."

"I will, son." Mack pulled out Jaycee's chair for her. "Give my regards to Miss Nicole and tell her not to forget her lunch date with Grandpa tomorrow."

Bud bent to kiss Jaycee on the cheek. "Try to stay out of trouble, Firecracker."

"No promises," she said.

Jess found the whole exchange intriguing, but Marjorie was looking a bit nonplussed.

Jaycee must've noticed because she said, "I'm afraid he wasn't joking about the probation. I had an unfortunate encounter in the pro shop with an employee who didn't know that Bud is married to a woman with no tolerance for ambitious bimbos."

Marjorie's expression transformed to one of amusement. "I think I know the woman you mean. Good for you."

Jess laughed. "I have to agree about bimbos. Sounds to me as if you were only performing a public service."

"Jaycee has always been her own woman." Mack gave her a fond smile. "And we wouldn't want her any other way."

Jaycee returned his smile just as fondly. "Well, it wouldn't do you any good if you did, but I'm glad you're okay with being the father-in-law of a charm school dropout and the poster child for anger management classes."

The whole time the waitress was taking their orders, Jess tried to wrap her mind around the idea of the radical woman across the table being a successful children's author, and she hoped it didn't show on her face. Jaycee wasn't at all what she'd expected, but Jess couldn't wait to find out more about her.

While they ate, Jaycee told them how her first book of stories was actually written as a result of her unhappy childhood, and she also had no qualms about admitting that the troublesome heroine in her new series was based on herself as a child. She really was an intriguing woman.

When the waitress returned for their dessert orders, Mack declined and instead invited Marjorie to take a stroll with him so Jaycee and Jess could talk shop in private.

"Say hello to Daddy for me if you run into him," Jess said before they left.

"Of course, dear." Marjorie smiled as she took her escort's arm. "Tell me, Mack. Do you by chance know the Heimlich maneuver?"

"I'm afraid not," he replied. "Is that a problem?"

"Not for me." Marjorie winked at Jess as they walked away.

"Well, that certainly smacked of something I need to know more about," Jaycee said. "My first love was journalism, so let's hear it."

Jess laughed as the waitress brought their coffee. "I'm afraid my mother's hoping to take advantage of Mr. Stanton's good looks so she can give my father a little payback for moving out." She paused to shake her head. "I can't believe I'm laughing about my parents' divorce, but it's actually brought my mother and me closer than I ever thought possible."

"No need to feel guilty about using Mack to rattle your father's cage," Jaycee said. "In fact, I'm sure the old scoundrel will be happy to fan the flames if they run into your dad."

"I guess I really shouldn't take sides," Jess said. "And I can sympathize with my father about some things. But I don't have any more tolerance for ambitious bimbos than you do, and it appears he left my mother for one."

"Men," Jaycee said with a scowl. "I've only known a handful worth keeping around, and my husband only falls into that category part of the time."

"Mine too," Jess said before she could stop herself. She looked at Jaycee sheepishly and added, "Ignore that. You definitely don't want to hear that morbid tale."

"Don't be so sure. What's he like?"

Jess looked into her coffee cup and sighed. "He's arrogant, self-centered, immature, and better looking than any man is entitled to be."

Jaycee's laughter drew several glances from neighboring diners. "You just described Bud to a T. You're not married to him too, are you?"

"No, Lee's a blond. Come to think of it, though, they are about the same height."

"Well, let me tell you the best way to handle a man like ours." Jaycee leaned forward and lowered her voice only slightly. "Make sure he knows that even though you like seeing his pretty face across the pillow from yours in the morning and need a daily dose of his body, you can take care of yourself just fine if he can't toe the line." She paused and looked thoughtful. "You know, I may get that stitched onto a throw pillow for my bed."

Jess laughed. "I'm not sure that philosophy will work the same for me as it does for you. I can't imagine anyone ever thinking you couldn't take care of yourself."

Jaycee's voice took on a reflective tone, and her fingers toyed with the lace doily on the table. "I'm a lot different than I used to be. My life took me down some roads I never expected to travel because of Bud, but I know everything happened for a reason and turned out for the best." She looked up at Jess and smiled. "It'd make a helluva book, that's for sure."

"I'm sure it would. I'd buy it."

"Maybe you could write it," Jaycee said. "With the names changed to protect the not-so-innocent, of course."

Jess shook her head. "I'm not sure I could ever write an entire book. All I've managed so far are a few short stories that I've never let anyone read."

Jaycee took a card from her purse. "Trust me, after you get your first good review, you'll be hooked and wanting everyone to read your work. Send your stories to me when you get home and I'll induct you into the Feedback Junkie Club."

"Okay, I'll do that." Jess took the card and put it in her pocket. "But I want you to promise you'll be honest and tell me what you really think."

"Don't worry, honest is all I know how to be. And anything that's on my mind eventually comes out of my mouth." She paused to laugh again. "Another slogan for my throw pillows. Now tell me what your blond hunk did to make you look so overwrought when you talk about him. And how long have you had trichotillomania?"

Jess almost spit her coffee across the table. "How did you know that?"

Jaycee nodded. "I can see the conscious effort you make to keep your hand away from your hair, and I recognize the competing responses you use."

Jess was grateful her chin didn't hit the edge of the table when her mouth fell open. "Oh my God. Do you have TTM, Jaycee?"

"No, my daughter does, but she pulled her lashes instead of her hair. Still, I know all about it. I'm happy to say she's been pull-free for three years thanks to Habit Reversal Training."

"Oh, isn't it a godsend? I hope I'll be able to thank Dr. Penzel in person someday."

Jaycee told her she intended to include a character with TTM in her next book and already had plans for speaking engagements to coincide with the next awareness campaign.

"That's so great to hear," Jess said. "So many people suffer in silence because they don't know how many others there are like them. I admire you so much for what you're doing, Jaycee. You're an amazing woman."

"Oh, stop with the goo-goo eyes," Jaycee said. "I'm just a mother who doesn't want anyone else's child being told they're mentally ill by idiot doctors who want to pass them off to a shrink. Trust me, the ones who tried to tell Bud and me that our daughter was crazy will think twice before they do that again. One of them still has a restraining order against me."

Jess laughed. "I'm going to love watching you give them hell about it, Jaycee."

"So does your hair pulling have anything to do with your marriage troubles?"

"No, that's one thing he's been wonderful about." Jess told her how Lee had defended Cara to her father and how supportive he'd always been for Lexie.

"I'm glad he's more than just a pretty face and a fine ass," Jaycee said. "So what does he do that would make you pull out your hair even if you didn't have TTM?"

Jess shook her head with a shrug. "Mostly it's because he gets himself confused with the big yellow thing in the sky around which the Earth rotates and all life depends."

Jaycee snickered. "Oh, yeah. I can definitely relate to that."

"To be honest, I know he doesn't intentionally act like a selfish jerk," Jess said. "I thought I'd finally come to grips with overlooking his faults, but now he's the one who's mad at me over a misunderstanding because he's jealous of a man I knew as a teenager."

"Oh my God, he and Bud must've been separated at birth. So this other guy—is there a legitimate reason your husband should worry about him?"

Jess waited until the waitress left after placing two slices of lemon meringue pie in front of them. "No. He's a sweet and caring man who just recently told me he's had feelings for me since we were in junior high, but we're only friends. He's probably a much better match for me than my husband, but he knows I have an incurable case of Lee-itis."

Jaycee took a bite of her pie and said, "Well, let me amend what I told you earlier about dealing with a man like ours. It's perfectly okay to cut him some slack for making stupid mistakes as long as you know he loves you and he's honestly trying. No matter how much of a badass I pretend to be, Bud has always been my safe harbor, and I wouldn't be the woman I am without him. As crazy as he makes me sometimes, he also makes me the best Jaycee I can be."

"I think I know what you mean. Thank you for everything, Jaycee. You've helped me more than you know."

"No problem. I was glad when Mack called and asked me to come, especially since it got me out of going to the photographer's with Bud and Nickie."

"Why didn't you want to go?" Jess asked. "Don't tell me you're camera shy."

"I'm not any kind of shy. But since I think weddings are a pretentious waste of money and couldn't talk my daughter into having a simple ceremony on the baseball field where she met her fiancé, Bud's grandmother hired a wedding planner. Seriously, the woman's life is in danger every time I have to be in the same room with her."

Jess laughed around a mouthful of pie. "Her name wouldn't be Amelia, would it?"

"God, yes," Jaycee said. "Do you know her?"

Jess nodded. "She did my sister's wedding. And if you want to get rid of her the day of the ceremony, just hide her headset. She'll have a stroke for sure and will have to be rushed to the hospital."

Jaycee high-fived her. "I knew I liked you. That's a much better idea than jacking her jaw, and Bud won't have to miss the reception to bail me out."

They saw Marjorie and Mack crossing the dining room toward them, and Jess could tell by the amused look on Marjorie's face that they had indeed run into her father and gotten the kind of reaction her mother had wanted. Since she didn't hear any approaching sirens, Jess hoped it meant her father was still among the living. She waited until they had said their goodbyes to Mack and Jaycee and were in the car on the drive back to her mother's house before she got the details of the encounter.

"Your father was just coming in from the cabana as

Mack and I were going out the door to the pool area," Marjorie said. "I do believe that if Bill's face had gone one shade darker red, it would have matched his shirt perfectly."

"Did you speak to each other?" Jess asked.

"I had no intention of saying a word to him," Marjorie replied with a lift of her chin, "but Mack was his usual courteous self. He said hello to your father and asked how the tournament was going for him. Bill grumbled something about an inexperienced caddy, then he made a snide remark about how he never knew I was such a golf enthusiast, seeing as how I'd never attended a tournament before."

Jess covered her mouth to keep from giggling. "What did you say to that?"

Marjorie kept her eyes on the road, but Jess could see the devilment in her expression. "I told him I still thought golf was incredibly boring, but I was delighted to find—contrary to my past experience—that some golfers were anything but."

Jess smiled and shook her head. "That's terrible, Mother. I'm so proud of you."

Marjorie laughed. "Oh, that's not the best part. Then your father tried to embarrass Mack by expressing his 'regret' about some business deal of Mack's that had fallen through. Without missing a beat, Mack told him that although he'd always been a risk taker who liked a vast and varied portfolio, he'd decided to concentrate on one or two choice acquisitions that had recently become available."

Jaycee had been right about Mack being a scoundrel, and Jess laughed. "Well, I'm not sure I'd like being referred to as an acquisition, but I *am* sure it must've put a burr in Daddy's boots."

"Don't worry, dear." Marjorie patted Jess's leg. "I have no intention of becoming one of Mack's acquisitions. He's far too much of a flirt for my taste, but your father doesn't need to know that. And I'm afraid Bill left in a huff before I had the chance to tell him you said hello."

"That's okay. I'll call him when I get back home. And you need to talk to Elise too, Mother."

"Whatever for?" Marjorie asked.

"You need to let her know you're getting along fine on your own. And you should also tell her you're glad she's there for Daddy, because you have *me*."

They smiled at each other, and Marjorie reached over to take Jess's hand. "And you have me as well, Jessica. Don't forget that."

****

Jess drove home the next morning in such high spirits that she actually felt a little guilty about her lack of anguish over her problems with Lee. She also couldn't help feeling a little proud of herself for not letting him dominate her thoughts and feelings to the exclusion of everything else the way he'd always done in the past. She and Marjorie had spent the rest of the visit mending their relationship even more, and Jess wasn't willing to give up the good mood she'd been in since discovering that she and her mother had quite a bit more in common than just their marriage troubles.

She'd done a lot of thinking before falling asleep the night before and had realized that ever since she'd begun focusing on her own pursuits and stopped obsessing over whether Lee cared about them or not, their relationship had actually improved. And she'd decided that she needed to concentrate on taking care of herself instead of resenting Lee or her mother for not meeting or understanding her needs. That was the only way she could claim any kind of real independence.

She also decided she wouldn't worry about what to say to Lee until she saw him. Of course she hoped he would believe her about Noah, but she'd be okay even if he didn't. Lee was the only man she loved or wanted and she intended to tell him that, but she wasn't going to apologize for Noah's friendship or promise to stay away from him just to soothe Lee's ego. She might be in love with a man who didn't share her interests and had only read *The Catcher in the Rye* because he thought it was about baseball, but that didn't mean she couldn't be friends with a man who knew the difference between *La Traviata* and *Les Miserables* and didn't think Rogers and Hammerstein made baking soda.

She laughed as she turned up the volume on the car's CD player. Michael Bublé was "Feeling Good" and singing gloriously about it, so she put her troubles aside and let him serenade her the rest of the way home. Honestly, the man could make aboriginal war chants sound heavenly. By the time she reached the Georgia line, she'd devised an ingenious plan for sneaking into his dressing room when she and her mother went to his concert together the following month. If it worked out as planned, she'd be able to forget about both Noah *and* Lee.

Chapter Twenty-One

In contrast to the animosity between Deb and Lee, Jess had always liked Howie and got along well with him. Her mood remained high after she got back to town and the three of them finished boxing up Deb's things to move them to Howie's new apartment. They had the truck loaded and ready to go by two o'clock, and from the look of the dark clouds gathering in the west, they'd made it just in time.

Jess rode in the U-haul with Deb and Howie and got them to stop at Gray's Gym where Trent worked so she could give him the extra key to her house. As grungy as she felt, no way was she going inside a gym full of muscle-bound men and disgustingly fit women, so she used Deb's cell phone to call Trent and let him know she was there. When he came out to the parking lot, Deb's eyes widened as she watched him walking toward the truck.

"Oh my God, Jess. He's got more muscle on him than the Incredible Hulk. Look at the size of those arms."

"He's a professional bodybuilder," Jess said with an amused look at Deb's awed expression. "According to Lee, he's won some major competitions."

Howie rolled his eyes. "Well, whoop-de-doo. Bet I could beat him in bowling."

Deb winked at Jess. "So do I, Sugarbear. And

you'd slaughter him in pinball."

Jess laughed as she got out of the truck. "Thanks for coming out to meet me, Trent. I didn't want to go in looking like this."

"I don't know what you're talking about." He tugged on a lock of her hair and chuckled. "You look really hot in a bandanna."

"Very funny." She shoved him and held out the key. "Here, you can just leave it on the kitchen counter when you're done. And tell Lee...no, never mind. I'll tell him myself when I see him."

He looked past her at the U-haul truck. "Moving to Stoneridge, huh? Nice digs."

"Yeah, and we've still got a lot of unloading to do before it rains, so we'd better run. See you later, Trent."

Deb eyed her suspiciously when she got back in the truck. "You want to tell me what that was all about?"

Jess shook her head. "Not now. Let's go before the bottom falls out of those clouds."

Howie's apartment turned out to be just across the parking lot from Noah's, and he was waiting for them on the sidewalk when they pulled up. While Howie backed the truck into a parking space in front of their apartment, Jess could tell Deb was checking Noah out thoroughly.

"Well, he's nice and tall," she said. "And he's got all his hair. You said he cooks too, right?"

Jess scowled at her. "Yes, and he's also the sweetest man in the world."

"Now him I know I could take," Howie said. "Maybe even in arm wrestling."

"Let's not get carried away, Sweetie Pie," Deb said. "I can beat you in that."

"Stop it, you two." Jess laughed and opened the door. "Come on so I can introduce you to him."

Noah walked up wearing a grin. "You should wear your hair like that more often, Jess. You look just like you did back in high school."

"Obviously, you're way overdue for an eye exam. Noah Hamilton, I want you to meet my best friend Deb Landry and her fiancé, Howie Parker."

Noah shook hands with Howie. "Happy to have you for neighbors. I think you'll find Stoneridge a great place to live."

Deb didn't release Noah's hand when she shook it. "God, you have the most incredible voice. Say something else."

He blushed and Jess rescued his hand. "He can recite the entire Constitution for you later, Deb. Right now we'd better get these boxes inside before we get wet."

As Noah walked beside Jess to the back of the truck, he said, "Actually, I only know the preamble to the Constitution. But I do know the entire Declaration of Independence."

"Doesn't surprise me a bit," she said.

He opened the back of the truck and climbed inside. "I'm sure you know how much I'm hoping that having your friends for neighbors will mean you'll be a frequent visitor here."

"Oh, I'll be around plenty." Jess accepted his hand to help her up. "In fact, maybe we can all get together sometime. Howie's a real character, and Deb will crack you up."

Noah's eyebrows rose slightly as he handed her one of the smaller boxes. "Would these get-togethers include your husband?"

Jess scoffed. "Not hardly. Lee and Deb get along like..." She paused a moment then smiled. "Like Hamilton and Burr."

"Oh." He nodded. "Have you heard from him again?"

"Only indirectly." She told him about Lee's call to Trent as they carried the boxes inside Deb and Howie's apartment. "I hope he'll be reasonable when he gets back, but I'm not going to beg or apologize when I haven't done anything wrong."

With all four of them working, they had the truck unloaded in less than an hour. Just as Jess and Noah were taking the last of the boxes from the back of the truck, the sound of squealing tires drew their attention toward the entrance of the complex. Jess's heart almost stopped when she saw Lee's Mustang peal in and screech to a stop at the curb beside the truck.

"Noah, go inside," she said as Lee jumped out and started toward them.

Noah didn't move, but Jess wasn't sure if it was bravery or paralyzing fear that held him immobile. She turned to yell at Lee but stopped when she saw the look on his face.

"For God's sake, Jess, don't do it! I finally get it, okay?"

"Lee, what are you—"

"Trent told me you were here." He stopped in front of her and grabbed both her hands without so much as a glance at Noah. "You have to let me show you that I finally figured it out, Jess. I know what you meant now."

"Well, I'm glad one of us knows," she said,

"because I don't have a clue what you're talking about."

"Remember when you asked me why I love you?" He looked down at her earnestly. "You told me you didn't want to be married to me unless I could give you the right answer, remember? Well, I know it now, Jess. It hit me in New York while I was so mad at you that I got falling-down drunk and went out to look for the trashiest women I could find so I could call and tell you about it."

"I don't want to hear any more!" She tried to free her hands but he wouldn't let them go.

"Yes you do. Listen to what I have to tell you and see if you still want to move in with him."

She heard a sharp intake of breath from Noah behind her, but she was glad he didn't say anything. Since Lee obviously had no intention of hurting Noah despite what he thought, Jess wanted to hear what he had to say before she corrected the misunderstanding.

"Fine, Lee. Tell me what you figured out while you were a drunken idiot."

"I think I should leave you two alone," Noah said.

"No, you can stay," Lee said, although he still didn't look at him. "In fact, I want you to hear this so you'll know why I'll never let you have her."

Deb and Howie came out of their apartment, and Deb said, "What's going on, Jess? You want me to call the cops on this riffraff?"

"You can hear it too, Broom Hilda," Lee said. "I want everybody to know it."

"It's okay, Deb." Jess found herself unable to look anywhere but Lee's face. "Let him talk."

He closed his eyes and took a deep breath before

looking at Jess again. "When I hung up with you Friday night, I was so mad at the thought of him alone with you at our house that I headed straight to the bar to get smashed, but I couldn't stop thinking about you long enough to even look at any of the women there. So after I was good and drunk, I went back to my room to call and tell you that at least one of us knew how to be faithful. When I found out you weren't home in the middle of the night, I really lost it. I trashed the room and called Trent to go get my stuff for me because I never wanted to see you again." He paused and held up his bandaged right hand. "I put my fist through the bathroom door in the hotel room."

Jess sighed. "Lee, this isn't proving anything except how immature you are."

"I know, baby, but I'm not done yet." He paused for another breath. "After I threw the phone out the window, I tripped over something and must've passed out for a few minutes. The first thing I saw when I opened my eyes was my wallet on the floor, open to your picture. I don't know how long I sat there holding it and bawling like a baby while I stared at you, but suddenly it hit me. I realized I'd never felt more miserable in my life, and even though it was all your fault and I wanted to hate you for it, I still loved you. That's when I knew what you've been talking about all along. It was like a light bulb went on in my head. You know, an epitome."

"Epiphany," Jess managed to say even though her heart was in her throat. "Keep talking, Lee."

"I finally *got* it, Jess. I always thought I loved you because you made me happy and believed in me and helped me accomplish all the things that were important to me. But there I was feeling the worst I'd ever felt in my life—even worse than when the doctor told me I couldn't play football anymore—and I still loved you. And I knew I'd go on loving you even if it was too late and you'd already left me for this guy. And that's not all." He reached in his pocket and withdrew a crumpled piece of paper covered with scribbled writing and what looked like bloodstains. "I wrote it all down so I wouldn't forget before I could tell you."

Deb snickered. "Oh, jeez. He brought crib notes."

"Shut up, Deb," Jess said. "What is that, Lee?"

"These are the things I'd miss the most if I lost you. They're the reasons I love you."

She wanted to tell him to go on, but she suddenly found it difficult to breathe. He opened the paper and stared at it, and she couldn't believe it when she saw his hands shaking. She couldn't remember ever seeing him nervous about anything before. And when he looked up at her again, she saw real fear on his face.

"Jessica Elaine Cassady, I love the way your eyes look like kaleidoscopes whenever you're in bright sunlight. I love the way you fit perfectly inside my arms when we're sleeping. I love the way our breathing always gets in sync when you lie next to me after we make love, and I love the way you put your ear over my heart like you're listening to my heartbeat. I love the way your lips are so perfect they look like somebody painted them with wine-colored paint. I love the way your skin feels like silk when it's next to mine, and I love your beautiful model feet that make the ones in the magazines look uglier than sin. I even love the way you talk to your stupid cat and ask her questions like you expect to get an answer. And I'd love you even if you pulled out all your hair and mine too."

He paused to wipe his eyes with the back of his hand.

"I don't know why it took me so long to wise up. Maybe I'm just stupid, or maybe you were right and I was too conceited to worry about other men before now. But ever since that night I saw you holding hands with this guy, I knew I'd better get my act together or I was gonna lose the best thing that ever happened to me. It just took me until now to figure out the right way to do it."

He paused again and pulled her hand to his heart.

"I love you more than anything in the world, and I'd rather stay here with you and cover Little League than lose you and cover the Braves. Say you'll stay with me and I'll give it all up tomorrow, because *nothing's* more important to me than you."

She could only stare at him through her own tears as she wondered how he'd managed to come up with all the right things to say, especially when she hadn't known herself what she needed to hear from him. He really *did* get it, and he'd figured it out all by himself. And how priceless was it that he'd done it after she'd finally decided she didn't need to hear it from him to believe it? She opened her mouth to tell him he didn't have to give up anything to keep her, but Deb moved beside him before Jess could say a word.

"Hell, Jess," she said. "That was the sweetest crap I've ever heard. Even I'd take him back after that. "

Jess laughed, and it helped her voice to work again. "Lee, I'm not the one moving in here, Deb and Howie are. How many times do I have to tell you that everything's not always about you?" She threw her arms around his neck and kissed him.

"But, I thought—"

"I know what you thought, and I'm sorry I made you so miserable over something that was just a misunderstanding. Noah and I are friends, and that's all we've ever been. You're the only man I'll ever love, and after the things you just said, you deserve to know that."

Noah put a hand on Jess's shoulder. "I guess you were right about him, Jess. He's a lot smarter than those guys you dated in high school."

Lee finally looked at him and smiled, although he pulled Jess a little closer to him. "Thanks, man. Sorry for all that stuff I said about breaking your face."

"No problem." Noah extended his hand. "Sorry for all the stuff I said about you to Jess's cat."

Chapter Twenty-Two

Jess and Lee celebrated their reunion for an hour after they got home, then they talked some more while they lay in each other's arms, a perfect fit just as Lee had pointed out.

"I meant what I said about the job, baby. I'll give it up if you want me to."

Jess shook her head. "I don't get to start being selfish just because you've stopped, Lee. I couldn't ask you to give up the job you've always wanted. I never really wanted you to give it up in the first place. I just wanted to be included in your decision to take it."

"It *is* a great job, but it's not the only thing I've always wanted."

"What do you mean?"

His fingers trailed lightly along her upper arm. "Ever since we went to my dad's grave on Father's Day, I've been having dreams about little bitty shoes and socks and somebody who calls me Daddy."

Jess sat up so she could look at his face. "The last time we talked about a baby, you said it belonged on a back burner."

"I know, but I think it's time we moved it up to the front." He pulled her down beside him again. "Think about it, baby. We owe it to the world to give it a couple of little Cassadys with their father's charm and athletic ability and their mother's brains and beautiful feet."

She laughed. "Oh, they'll be set for life with those attributes."

He laughed with her, then his face sobered. "Seriously, Jess. I had another revelation while I was drunk and bawling over you. I just didn't want to say anything about it in front of your friends."

"What was it, Lee?"

"You know the picture next to yours in my wallet is the one of me and my dad at my graduation. I was looking at it and wishing he was here to tell me what to do, and I remembered something that happened when I was a little kid, probably only three or four years old. I swear, Jess, it was like my dad was sending me a message to straighten me out."

"What did you remember?"

He didn't answer right away, and she could tell he was trying not to cry.

"My dad came home from work one day, so worn out that he fell asleep in his chair in the middle of taking off his shoes. I tried to take off his other shoe for him, and my mom got on to me for waking him up. I remember my dad holding me on his lap and telling my mom not to ever scold me for bothering him, because I was the reason he worked so hard in the first place. And he said the best part of his day was seeing me when he got home."

"I can hear your dad saying those words, Lee."

"I know. And while I was looking at the picture of him and me, I realized that the first thing I ever wanted to be and my biggest goal in life has always been to be like my dad—a man who loved his wife and kids more than anything in the world. He worked so hard for us all his life, and I owe it to him to be the same kind of man he was. I looked at his picture in my hand and promised him that if you'd take me back, I'd be the best husband and father I could be."

He looked into Jess's eyes, and she could see the tears that he wasn't trying to hide.

"My dad told me once that he felt like the richest man in the world because he had a family who loved him and loved each other, and that's what I want too, baby. I want a family with you like the one I grew up in, and I want to be the kind of father I had. One who was always there when I needed him and behind me in everything I did. That's way more important to me than any by-line or money or prestige."

Jess put her hand on his cheek. "I don't know how you got so smart all of a sudden, but I'm glad you did."

"Maybe I knocked something loose in my head when I passed out." He wiped his eyes and smiled. "You probably could've saved us both a lot of trouble if you'd just conked me over the head with something a long time ago."

She laughed. "I'll keep that in mind if you give me any problems in the future."

"So what do you say, Jess?" He rolled over and pulled her on top of him. "Ready to get started on those little Cassadys right now?"

She ran her hand over his chest. "I'm glad you've figured out the important things, Lee, but I don't want you to give up this job and regret it later on. Even if we started trying now, we wouldn't have any little Cassadys before next year, so why don't you take the job for at least one baseball season?"

He tucked her hair behind her ear. "You don't

think I'd leave you here by yourself while you're pregnant, do you? Maybe I used to be that selfish, but I'm not that guy anymore."

"But what if I had someone here with me so you wouldn't need to worry while you were gone?"

"Like who?"

"My mother."

He scoffed. "Oh, sure. And I guess you'd have the prison matrons taking care of you after the murder, so you still wouldn't be alone. Yeah, it could work."

She laughed and told him about her parents' divorce, her trip to Tampa, and her new relationship with her mother.

"Wow, that's great, baby," he said. "It's about time your mother realized what an incredible daughter she has." He turned over again and began kissing her neck. "And since this means you'll have somebody to stay with you on baby watch, I definitely think we should get started right now on making the little rugrat."

She slid her hands over the muscles in his back and down the delectable curve of her favorite part of his anatomy. "Well, okay. If you think—"

The ringing phone interrupted her.

Lee raised up on one elbow and gave her a wry smile. "Why don't we let the machine get that?"

"Good idea." She pulled him back down.

He resumed kissing her, but when the caller identified herself as an editor with *The Georgia Review*, his head jerked up again.

"Wait, Jess! We need to take this call!"

"*What?* Lee, you just told me—"

"Trust me, baby. You won't be sorry."

The caller had hung up by then, and Jess couldn't

believe it when Lee got up to replay the message. "Lee, how can you do this after everything you said to me? Was it all just a lie?"

"No, baby." He wrote down the name and phone number. "But this call is different."

She threw a pillow at him. "Why? What's so damn important about it?"

He turned to look at her with an exasperated sigh. "Jess, this call is for *you*. I submitted one of your short stories to this magazine."

"What are you talking about?" She scrambled across the bed and snatched the paper from his hands. "I haven't shown you any of my stories!"

"Remember that night I got drunk and slept on the couch? You told me the next morning that you wrote short stories, so after you got mad at me and stormed off to get in the shower, I booted up your computer and printed out the one about the girl who offed her boyfriend."

She smacked him on the chest. "You had no right to do that without my permission! You are such a—"

"It's a helluva story, baby."

She stopped with her hand in mid-smack. "You really think so?"

He grinned. "Oh, yeah. And I knew you'd never submit it anywhere if you were too chicken to even let *me* read it. Since I've got enough guts for both of us, I bought a copy of the *Writer's Market* and sent it to some magazines where it'd be a good fit."

"Lee, it was still incredibly presumptuous of you to do something like that." She suppressed her smile a few seconds longer before she threw her arms around his neck and hugged him. "And I'm so glad you're such an arrogant jerk."

"For real, Jess. I don't understand why you never showed them to anyone before." He sat on the bed and pulled her onto his lap. "You know I'm not much of a fiction reader, but your stuff was like watching a movie. I could see everything that was happening. And it kind of creeped me out too."

"Really? Why?"

He gave her a wary look. "You're not planning to push me into a lake, are you?"

She rolled her eyes. "Stop trying to make this about you and tell me exactly what you thought about it. Did you like the foreshadowing? Was I too obvious about what was going on from the beginning? Did you feel for the girl?"

She grilled him until she was satisfied, then she fell back onto the bed and kicked her feet in delight.

"Jaycee was right—I'm hooked! I can't wait to hear what she thinks about my stories."

"Who's Jaycee?"

"She's a published writer my mother introduced me to in Tampa, and she's one of the most amazing, inspiring women I've ever met." She told him about Jaycee's books, her plans for a character with TTM, and her upcoming interviews about it.

"You're amazing and inspiring too, Jess. Look at all you've done for Lexie and Cara. You should go on TV with her to show everybody that people with TTM can be beautiful and talented and smart. I bet it would inspire a lot of people."

"That's not a bad idea, Lee. Maybe I'll keep you around for a while after all."

"Yeah, like you have any choice," he said. "You're

stuck with me for life."

She arched an eyebrow. "Don't be so sure about that. If the past few months have taught me anything, it's that I can survive on my own if I have to. I might like seeing your pretty face across the pillow from mine in the morning and need a daily dose of your body, but I can get along just fine if you can't toe the line." She struggled not to laugh at her use of Jaycee's slogan.

"Oh, really?" He pushed her backward and lay on top of her. "Well, why don't we give you a booster shot of my body right now and get to work on those little Cassadys we were discussing earlier?"

She tried to wriggle out from under him. "Okay, but let me just listen to that message from the magazine editor first."

"Nope." He pinned her hands to the bed and lowered his lips to her neck. "We were in the middle of something important, and we shouldn't let any stupid phone calls interrupt us."

"But, Lee, let me just—"

"Uh-uh. No way, Mrs. Cassady. We have to keep our priorities straight here. Nothing's more important than this." His mouth traveled up to her earlobe.

"This isn't fair." She laughed and struggled fruitlessly.

"Oh yes it is. From now on, this is the top priority for both of us. We're working toward a common goal here and have to be equally committed to it. Synergy, just like you wanted."

"Symmetry, Lee." She stopped struggling and switched to kissing. "And you're right. This is exactly what I want."

A word about the author...

Formerly the senior editor for Champagne Books, Joyce now writes full time and does freelance editing. She just contracted elsewhere for a three-book YA series and is working on two others. She's a member of SCBWI and is active in her local writers' guild.

Joyce has lived all her life on the Alabama Gulf Coast, she has three gifted children, and she's been married for thirty years to the love of her life.

Find her at:

http://joycescarbrough.blogspot.com

Thank you for purchasing
this publication of The Wild Rose Press, Inc.
For other wonderful stories of romance,
please visit our on-line bookstore at
www.thewildrosepress.com.

For questions or more information
contact us at
info@thewildrosepress.com.

The Wild Rose Press, Inc.
www.thewildrosepress.com

To visit with authors of
The Wild Rose Press, Inc.
join our yahoo loop at
http://groups.yahoo.com/group/thewildrosepress/

www.ingramcontent.com/pod-product-compliance
Lightning Source LLC
Chambersburg PA
CBHW070052260626
47160CB00004B/1189